Gillian Slovo was born in Johannesburg in 1952 and came to England in 1964. She has worked as a writer, journalist and film producer. She has written three other Kate Baeier mysteries: *Morbid Symptoms*, *Death by Analysis* (The Women's Press, 1986) and, the latest, *Catnap*. Her other works are *Ties of Blood*, *Betrayal* and *Façade*. She lives in North London with her partner and daughter.

Also by Gillian Slovo from The Women's Press:

Death by Analysis (1986)

GILLIAN SLOVO

DEATH comes
STACCATO

First published by The Women's Press Ltd, 1987
A member of the Namara Group
34 Great Sutton Street, London EC1V 0DX

Reprinted 1994

British Library Cataloguing-in-Publication Data
Slovo, Gillian
   Death comes staccato
   I. Title
   823[F]   PR6069.L56

ISBN 0 7043 4055 0

Printed and bound in Great Britain by BPCC Paperbacks Ltd,
Aylesbury, Bucks

One

They lived at the back of Selfridges in one of those buildings where cost was the last thing on the interior decorator's mind. They had everything money can buy, including the kind of doorman who looks you up and down, assessing whether to escort you up. Me, he decided to escort. He smiled blandly as he pointed to a choice of two four-seaters covered in yellow velvet which stood opposite his desk. I saw the smile vanish as he turned away to use the phone. While he muttered into the receiver he kept a wary eye on me. Perhaps he was scared that I'd run away with the velvet.

When his colleague arrived, the doorman gestured to the lift. I got in and he followed me. I held my breath. The lift was small, lined in red brocade and plush. It gave me claustrophobia. There was nowhere to look and nothing to do as it made silent, but slow, progress. The doorman solved the problem by rubbing at the shiny gold buttons on his blue jacket.

The lift stopped without seeming to. It gave off a quiet ping and the doors opened. The doorman didn't get out. He stood there watching, his hands still working at his buttons, as I went to number 52.

He was still watching when I pressed the bell to produce four subtle chimes. The door was opened by a maid dressed in a short black and white number. She gave me a quick smile and then she nodded at the doorman. I heard the lift ping again.

The maid stepped to one side revealing the interior. I

1

found myself facing a long corridor carpeted in thick white pile. The walls were lined by mirrors as was the ceiling. The whole effect was of an ice palace.

The maid dodged neatly in front of me. She walked on and I followed her. When she was halfway down the hallway she stopped abruptly. She pressed at the mirror. It swung open revealing a vast room.

The maid pointed into the space, and I stepped through the opening. She waited until I had gone a few feet and then she pushed another bit of the mirror. The door swung shut behind me.

It was a big room. At first I thought that the mirrors had distorted my perceptions, so big did it seem. But I blinked a couple of times and the ballroom proportions remained. So did the music. It was a crescendo of piano notes that swelled and swayed, filling the room with passion.

The music stretched ahead and beyond me. It jarred with the soft light of sunset which filtered in through the floor-to-ceiling windows, and it bounced off the polished floorboards. It was music of defiance, of rebellion and of torment. It was music not meant for a stranger's ear.

It was coming from a grand piano that was placed at one end of the massive room. I took a step towards it. The music ceased abruptly. I heard the sound of wood touching ivory before a young woman stepped out from behind the piano.

She was dressed in a black silk evening dress, cut low on her chest to show off soft shoulders. Grouped loosely round her straight white neck was a row of sparklers which flashed against her skin. Her face was milky white, broken by a delicate flush of pink in her cheeks. It was fading now and I guessed it had been brought on by the music. Her black eyes flashed in their deep sétting, her eyebrows dark and feathery above them. Her thick black hair was piled high on her head and topped by a further ring of diamonds. She was an image of wealth and sophistication. She must have been all of seventeen. She made me feel twelve, and a clumsy twelve at that.

2

She'd reached me now and her hand met mine. Before she withdrew it I noticed how cold it was.

'Kate Baeier,' she said. 'How good of you to come.'

'That was some playing.'

She got no pleasure from my compliment. A fleeting frown crossed her forehead and I noticed the lines that were already etched there. She pointed to the far end of the room.

We walked towards a ring of sofas which was tucked into an alcove, itself larger than my whole living room. The sofas were fawn leather and as comfortable as sofas can get. I sank into one and watched my companion do the same.

There was a slight sound behind us. The woman opposite me shook her head. I turned and was just in time to see the retreating back of the maid.

When I turned round again I saw that the girl was watching me intently. She looked worried about something, but when she noticed that I'd noticed, she smiled. I couldn't help thinking it was a brave smile.

'I'm Alicia Weatherby,' she said. 'I'm so pleased you could come so promptly.'

I nodded. And waited. She hadn't told me anything worth repeating on the phone and I was waiting to see if she would tell me now.

She gestured at her costume and laughed deprecatingly. 'I know it's a trifle early for this,' she said, 'but I'm performing later and I didn't want to interrupt our meeting to change.'

'You play piano?' I asked.

She looked startled, frightened even. 'Oh no,' she said, 'my instrument's the violin.'

I frowned at the memory of the music I'd just heard. My own training was not classical, but it hadn't been hard to tell that Alicia was good. And not only was she good, she played with a passion that could one day make her better, even great.

She saw my frown.

'I tinker on the piano,' she explained. 'But my mother doesn't think it's entirely suitable and I agree. Not many

3

people succeed as pianists. It's safer in the violin section.'

I took in the wealth that surrounded her and I wondered why she needed to worry about security. She started to say something but stopped herself abruptly. The sound that I'd learned to associate with the door opening had interrupted her. On second thoughts, I might have heard the sound but I might just have known about it because of the transformation that came over the girl's features.

It was as if she suddenly shrank into herself, losing her vibrancy. Her eyes dulled, her mouth closed and her lips tightened petulantly. Away flooded the confidence and with it the sophistication. Now she was just a little girl in a dress too old for her.

The woman whose entrance had had such a startling effect on my companion knew how to get attention. At a guess she was in her middle forties, but this was purely based on a glance at her hands. Elsewhere her skin was as smooth as the seventeen-year-old's. Her beige flannel suit hugged close to a body which had kept its trim shape. Her hair was blond and immaculate and if it was dyed there was no way I could tell.

She came and sat down next to me without ruffling the air around us. She smiled and ignored my outstretched hand in so graceful a fashion that she couldn't possibly have given offence. She sank back into the leather as if she were really letting go, but even when relaxed she gave the impression that she was ready to move at a second's notice.

Her voice was coolly modulated but it had an edge to it.

'I see you and my daughter have already become acquainted,' she said. 'Unfortunate that I wasn't informed of your presence. I'm sure it would have saved us valuable time.'

She looked across at her daughter and seemed gratified when she saw the girl blanch. Then her eyes flashed from Alicia to the empty coffee table beside me. She frowned. She stretched to the end of the sofa and pressed something. The maid came almost immediately. She stood to attention.

'Why wasn't our guest offered refreshment?' Marion

4

Weatherby asked.

The maid glanced at the girl. I saw a pleading look cross back to her. I wasn't the only one to catch the exchange. Mrs Weatherby smiled. 'Tea, I think,' she said.

The maid padded off. Mrs Weatherby turned her charm back on me.

'Our entire establishment is in uproar when Alicia performs,' she said. 'She informs me that this is one of the penalties of the life. However, there must be some satisfaction in getting one's every wish met, don't you think?'

I was saved from answering by the return of the jet-propelled maid. She was carrying a laden tray. She placed it on the table in front of Mrs Weatherby, dropped an almost inperceptible curtsey, and left.

Mrs Weatherby dispensed tea without denting the silence. Only when Alicia stretched forward to receive her bone china cup did I hear the tinkle of crockery.

I shook my head as a small plate of chocolate affairs was passed my way.

'No thanks,' I said.

'How sensible,' Mrs Weatherby said, and put the plate back on the table. Alicia stretched forward and took one of the chocolates.

'The appetites of youth,' Mrs Weatherby said, 'can often become the vices of old age. Or the luggage.'

She patted her flat stomach. I nodded my appreciation of it. That seemed to satisfy her. She put down her cup and leaned forward.

'Alicia and I have become somewhat perturbed of late,' she said. 'That is our reason for contacting you.'

Again I nodded. An understanding nod this time. I was beginning to wish she would get to the point. I was beginning to want to leave the room. I was beginning to sympathise with Alicia's look as her mother had entered.

Mrs Weatherby was no mindreader. She carried on blithely.

'My daughter is a musician,' she said. 'Rather a fine one at

5

that. She is often required to perform with her school orchestra. And at other youth performances. She has recently been awarded the singular honour of being chosen for the ECYO.'

'European Community Youth Orchestra,' Alicia said.

'I'm sure Miss Bazes knows all about that, dear,' her mother smiled through her polished teeth.

'You didn't,' Alicia replied.

'Baeier,' I said.

Mrs Weatherby chose to ignore us both.

'Such activity is bound to bring with it a certain notoriety. Alicia is occasionally bothered by the jealous colleague or the over-enthusiastic fan. But recently there has been a more worrying development.'

She paused to check that my breath was bated. It was. I was experimenting to see whether I could hold it longer than she could take to get to the point. She won. I breathed out and she carried on.

'For the past month my daughter has noticed a certain person in the audience. A person who watches her with excessive avidity.'

'A man?' I asked.

'A lone man,' Mrs Weatherby said. 'Alicia feels that his interest is somewhat unhealthy. She feels that he is watching her in particular.'

'He *is* watching,' Alicia interrupted. Her voice sounded childish after the modulated tones of her mother.

'And I see no reason to doubt Alicia,' Mrs Weatherby carried on. 'She is a sensible girl. I have made sure of that. I believe that this man exists.'

'You've never noticed him yourself?'

Mrs Weatherby frowned. 'I never attend Alicia's performances,' she said. 'She says I make her nervous.'

'And you don't know who the man is?' I asked Alicia.

She shook her head miserably. All sparkle had gone from her face. She looked tired out.

'How can I help?' I asked.

6

'We would like you to attend her concerts,' Mrs Weatherby answered, 'and identify the man. Find out what he's doing there: why he is interested in Alicia; whether he represents a threat to my daughter.'

'And then report back?' I asked.

Mrs Weatherby smoothed a non-existent crease from her skirt.

'That would be best,' she said.

She spoke as one used to getting her own way. Her face closed; she'd had her say.

I thought about my next question. It was a question that had been on my mind ever since I'd stepped into the sofaed entrance hall of the building and seen the doorman's uniform. It was a question that had become more necessary when I saw the maid and which had been enlarged in the corridor of mirrors. It was a question that I knew could lose me this job just when I could have done with some private work, but it was also one that I needed to ask. It was a question based on one simple fact of life – these people weren't my style and if there was one thing I knew for sure, I certainly wasn't theirs.

'Who recommended me to you?' I asked.

'Alicia located you,' Mrs Weatherby answered.

I looked at Alicia. I saw a plea for silence in her eyes. I smiled at her and then at Mrs Weatherby and we all relaxed. Not for long, though. Mrs Weatherby looked pointedly at the gold watch that circled her thin wrist.

'Time to get ready, darling,' she said, 'with those finger exercises.'

Alicia got up. So did her mother. I had no choice. I followed suit. Mrs Weatherby reached into the pocket of her jacket and brought out a crisp piece of paper.

'This is a list of Alicia's venues,' she said. 'I suggest you start at St James's tomorrow night. I understand that you will require expenses on top of your daily fee. I am quite prepared to cover reasonable expenditure, but I would warn you against taking advantage of me.'

7

The speech was more routine than threatening. It gave her time to guide me to the front door. She opened it and then moved away a fraction so I couldn't shake her hand. She nodded briskly. Business over, she wasn't going to waste any more of her smiles.

As soon as I was out the door closed behind me. I rode the silent elevator down. The doorman was in his kiosk when I reached the ground floor. He watched me step out and make my way towards the front door. I nodded at him, just for the hell of it. I think he nodded back but I could have been imagining it.

Two

I certainly wasn't imagining the chaos that greeted my eyes when I stepped into the office. I stood by the door and stared in amazement. It was hard to believe that one person could cope with so much disturbance around herself, even if she was Carmen. On second thoughts I take that back: Carmen is unique.

When I arrived she was stretched between two phones, one cradled precariously on her shoulder. She alternated chat between each receiver, using a spare hand to write notes. Her desk was covered in piles of papers which, I was convinced, stayed put only by defying the laws of gravity. As far as I was concerned they also defied the laws of logic. How anybody could cope with so complicated a mess and still keep operating had always been a mystery to me.

But Carmen was not just anybody. She was unique – a model of efficiency who could locate the smallest scrap from beneath the jumble of documents. She laughed at me when I tried to persuade her to clear up her mess. She told me that I was growing compulsive in my middle age and that, given the chance, I would clean the office so effectively that there'd be nothing left. In the end we compromised. I kept my comments to myself while she guaranteed to keep her chaos well away from my desk.

Carmen could manage a lot but even she was floored when the third phone started ringing.

'I'll get it,' I said and looked at her questioningly.

'Target Employment,' she mouthed and then went back to her conversations.

I reached for the phone and picked up the receiver.

'Target Employment,' I sang in my finest secretarial manner.

'Mr Mason, please,' said the modulated voice on the other end.

'Who can I say is calling?' I asked.

'Mr Bliss, Pharmaceutical Alloys.'

I covered the mouth-piece and got Carmen's attention.

'Pharmaceutical Alloys,' I said.

'Wrong lead,' she said. 'Tell them Mr Mason's out.'

I told the woman on the other end and she said not to bother with a message. She put down the phone abruptly.

Carmen had finished both her conversations simultaneously and she was looking at me expectantly.

'Mason's a new one on me,' I said.

'I used him temporarily,' Carmen said, 'but he got in the way so I ditched him. Want some coffee?'

I nodded and sat down on one of our comfortable client's chairs. I watched while Carmen got up and stretched the phone pose out of her cricked neck. She was standing against the light and the sun shone through her thick Afro and on to her reddish brown face.

She was a tall woman, and a strong one with it. Life had been hard for Carmen but she never showed it: instead of bending from the strain it was as if she'd grown strong from combating it. Sometimes I'd look at her six-year-old daughter Kaya, so full of life and energy, and imagine Carmen like that: a person who could allow her charm and her loud laugh to greet the world unprotected. Kaya, I knew, had learned those qualities from Carmen, but the adult woman had been forced to hide what she had taught the child to express.

I'd met Carmen by chance. I was investigating the murder of a therapist and I discovered that a young friend of hers had been witness to the death. It had not been a happy conjunction of events – her friend was eventually also killed. It wasn't the best of circumstances in which to start a friendship but I'd warmed to Carmen at first sight. After it was all over we agreed to keep in touch.

Nothing more might have come from it if not for the rush of work that unexpectedly landed on my desk. Originally in a position of having to supplement the detective work I enjoyed with the journalism that bored me, I suddenly found myself unable to cope with the demands for investigation.

I owed it all, indirectly, to the Greater London Council. Before it was abolished, the GLC had initiated a number of new work practices. Contract compliance – the process of checking that the enormous number of firms that supplied it were prepared to go along with its anti-racist, anti-sexist policies – was one of them.

After the GLC's demise, several other London boroughs had continued the policy. They found that it was arduous work checking on these firms who, naturally enough, were not always completely honest. I had managed to get an initial contract to do some of the groundwork, and once that was successfully concluded I had been deluged with similar requests. I ended up with more work than I could possibly handle on my own. I looked around for someone to work with.

Carmen was the obvious choice. She was unemployed, canny and completely unafraid of authority. And she had one other quality which made her invaluable: she knew how to persuade, intimidate and charm information from people of widely different backgrounds.

Somehow when Carmen was around, people seemed to feel the urge to spill their life stories. I think it must have been something about her detached but real interest which made people feel that they were important enough to be heard but not too important to be indulged.

After a few initial hiccups we'd established a good working relationship that now only occasionally became frayed at the edges. I had wanted a partner: Carmen left me in no doubt that she wasn't willing to oblige. Instead she got me to agree that I was the boss and she made sure that I never forgot it. It wasn't maliciously done – it was just that Carmen saw quickly

11

the pitfalls inherent in a messy division of labour and she would not tolerate any blurring of roles. She said I had chosen to start the agency: she took the job as a fill-in and didn't want to be tied to it.

It was a system that worked pretty well. Although Carmen was nominally my employee I made no attempt to supervise her. She didn't need that kind of help. She invented a hundred different ways of ferreting out information, including a series of aliases – Target Employment being only one of many – and she never forgot which one she'd given to which person. She had few doubts about her own competence and, after a few weeks of working alongside her, neither had I.

We'd taken an early decision to divide the assignments so that we wouldn't continually be tripping over each other. I raised the money and, as Carmen often repeated, got to worry about it. I spoke to our employers and fought over the contracts. I finalised the reports and presented them – something I had in fact been trying to push Carmen to do. So far I hadn't succeeded. She kept saying that she didn't have the wardrobe or the accent or, when it came down to it, the patience.

Carmen did much of the groundwork. She compiled the statistics, collected background information, delved into the details and generally immersed herself in the entire history of a firm under investigation. All this kept her pretty busy.

The other side of the business, the private jobs which came my way, were mine alone. Carmen resolutely avoided them, labelling them *petit bourgeois*. She was prepared to help when I was desperately overloaded, she would listen and comment when I got confused, but she never took them on herself. When I questioned her about her attitude she dismissed me by stating that she had no time for the pain of the individual life stories that I stumbled across.

Now she laughed out loud when I told her about the Weatherbys.

'Minder to the aristocracy,' she said. 'Makes a change I suppose.'

'Not sure about your class breakdown,' I replied. 'The place stank of new, not old, money. Can't see the mirror effect in an old country mansion.'

Carmen looked at me speculatively. 'Want me to find out where they get it from then?'

I nodded. 'And it would be good to know whether there's a Mr Weatherby or other male presence.'

Carmen made a note which she shoved in the general direction of what had once been her in-tray. If she saw my involuntary shake of the head at the mess, she ignored it. She reached on top of another pile and pulled down a clipboard.

'Most everything's under control,' she said. 'Just the report writing, and I've put all the details on your desk. Only item outstanding on this week's haul is Mately's.'

I looked up from where I had been leafing through Carmen's notes. 'Mately's?'

'Makes radio parts using new techniques. Front-runner as a small business. Talk of being competitive with Hong Kong which says something about the wage levels. Got a lot of YOPS kids working there. The firm was up for an ILEA contract and we were doing the usual investigation into their employment practices.'

'So?'

'So nothing,' Carmen said. 'Except that I'm having difficulty finding anything out and when that happens I begin to get suspicious. Nothing concrete. Just a feeling.'

'Your feelings are usually dead accurate,' I said. 'What have you tried?'

'Everything.'

It came out abruptly. I glanced at her. She was showing an uncharacteristic defeatism over this one and I wondered why. It hadn't looked particularly difficult. Perhaps, I thought, something else was worrying her.

I concentrated on the problem at hand. 'Let's do the checklist,' I suggested. Carmen and I often did this when we got stuck: going over the usual ground, assuring ourselves that something obvious had not been overlooked.

'Accounts?'

'Attached to my notes. Nothing out of the ordinary.'

'Managed by?'

'Jarvis – Gordon Jarvis. He's also the owner. He makes a good living out of his expense account but, as we say, that's between him . . .'

' . . . and the Inland Revenue,' I finished. 'Have you seen him?'

'Heard his voice. It's loud. I got fobbed off by an underling who assured me that Mately's was careful to abide by any anti-sexist, anti-racist practices you can name.'

'And you didn't believe him?'

'When I questioned him he spent a lot of time covering up for the fact that he didn't know what they were.'

'Other avenues?'

'I applied for a job using a false name. Got turned down without an interview which means they couldn't be said to have done it because I'm black.'

'Wages?'

'Abysmal. But nothing wrong there.'

I knew what she meant. That was her shorthand for saying that however low the wages were they conformed with the minimum and that women and men got paid the same for the same job.

'What about the employees?'

'Well,' Carmen said slowly, her face beginning to clear. 'That must be it. I couldn't get a word out of any of them.'

When she said that I also understood. If Carmen couldn't get anybody to talk then either absolutely nothing ever happened in their lives, or else something was being concealed.

'I'll get back on it,' Carmen said. 'In the meantime I think you should see Jarvis. I'll set it up.' She picked up the phone and dialled a number. She spoke briefly. When she put the receiver down she nodded in my direction. 'Tomorrow at eleven. See what your impressions are.'

'Will do,' I said. 'Anything else?'

14

'Someone called Archie phoned. Sounded stoned. Where did you find him?'

'On the floor of the stock exchange,' I said. 'That was before he moved into the money markets. He's the Left's only genuine jobber and at thirty he's getting a bit old for the trade.'

'Sounds like it,' Carmen said. 'The yawns were coming loud and fast over the phone. Said he'd been up all night switching money. He advised me to get out of yen fast. He also said that you were right – IBM is very interested in the Hardwick PC.'

I nodded and sighed. I turned to the phone on my desk and got hold of Jonathan Blenter, owner of the newly established Hardwick computers. Jonathan was a bright computing graduate who'd decided to start his own firm, positive that he could produce a personal computer which would perform as well as any in the market but for half the price.

It was a good idea but it was beginning to look like it would never get off the ground. Jonathan had enough money to develop the prototype but he needed much more before he could go into production. And that was where he came unstuck. He couldn't raise the capital anywhere.

He'd tried a variety of sources, each more desperate than the last, and was fobbed off by every one of them. It took him a long time to give up entirely but, when he did, he insisted on searching out the reasons for his failure. He'd come to me for help in finding out why there'd been so much resistance to his product.

I'd done a bit of preliminary investigation until I thought I had a pretty good idea as to what had happened. I went to Archie to check out my suspicions and his return call confirmed them.

Jonathan answered on the second ring. Never the most enthusiastic of people, that day he sounded positively suicidal.

'Jonathan,' I said, 'it's Kate. We were right. IBM is interested in your PC . . . Nobody's keen to invest in what

15

looks like an imminent takeover bid.'

My first fears were confirmed. Jonathan's voice dropped a tone lower.

'That's it then,' he said. 'Might as well close up shop.'

I felt a flash of irritation. I knew I wasn't supposed to get involved with my clients but Jonathan's passivity had always annoyed me.

The irritation showed in my voice. 'Hang on,' I said, 'and try and make something from a takeover.'

'Make what?' Jonathan muttered.

'Money,' I said. 'Capital for the next venture. They're playing the game of driving you out before you're even established. It's cheaper for them that way. But if you can hold out, there'll come a time when they make an offer. That way you'll get something.'

Jonathan didn't sound impressed.

'Yeah,' he said, 'I'll think about it. Can't say I have the energy.'

We said our goodbyes and we hung up. The irritation I'd felt had turned on me – changing into slight distaste and a generalised feeling of dissatisfaction. 'If you can't take the heat get out of the pot,' I muttered.

'This business is ruining me,' I said aloud to Carmen. 'I've started giving survival lessons to small capitalists.'

Carmen smiled. 'That's the eighties for you,' she said, 'added to the fact that Jonathan Blenter would get up anybody's nose.'

'Suppose so,' I said. 'I'm off. Coming?'

Carmen shook her head.

'Kaya's with a friend, so I'll catch up on my paperwork,' she said.

I left her sitting at the desk, frowning in concentration.

Matthew, Sam's nine-year-old son, was at the word processor when I got home. He was hunched over it, and angry.

'I k d-ed and nothing happened,' he said by way of greeting.

'Probably mis-typed,' I said. 'Try again.'

'I never type wrong,' Matthew snapped back while punching at the keyboard once more. There was a short silence as the computer clicked on and off once and his file was saved. Matthew wouldn't look up, so I didn't get to say that I told him so. Instead he pressed at the disk drive and busied himself tidying away his growing array of disks.

I left him to it and went to find Sam who had taken refuge from modern technology in the kitchen. The computer was courtesy of Sam's college – he'd brought it home to perform some kind of elaborate calculations, but Matthew had immediately colonised the machine and I had a sneaking suspicion that Sam was only too pleased to give it up. Certainly there in the kitchen, scratching at a piece of paper with a blunt pencil, Sam looked as if he was in his element.

I went up behind him and kissed the top of his head. He sort of shrugged an acknowledgment but apart from that he didn't do much. It wasn't an uncharacteristic greeting. Sam, who I'd been with for seven years, had perfected an air of abstraction. When I'd first noticed it I'd thought it was phoney – I was convinced that he could snap out of it should the need arise. But I'd long since learned that I was wrong: if he was in one of his trances all I could do was wait it out. I sighed loudly and switched on the kettle. A cup of coffee might give me the energy that the boys certainly weren't interested in supplying.

The water had all but dripped through the filter when Sam came to. He looked up and gave me a broad smile.

'Hello, darling,' he said. 'I didn't hear you come in.'

'I noticed,' I said. I poured him a cup and pushed it towards him.

'Rough day?' he asked.

I told him about it which took all of five minutes and then we set to preparing the meal. In the distance the sound of car chases through American streets had taken the place of computer bleeps. Every now and then Matthew would wander into the kichen, involve us in one of his nine-year-old

17

conversations about life and pocket money and then, when we were truly immersed in the morality of it all, he would exit, leaving us with a vague feeling that we had been taken for a ride. He did this all evening. When he'd gone to bed we looked in relief at each other.

'What brought that on?' I asked.

Sam shrugged. 'Been like that since I picked him up. I guess it's just the strain of full-time education. Plus the humiliation of losing the inter-Hackney chess semi-finals. If the team hadn't been entirely composed of little boys, there would have been weeping in the aisles.'

'What happened to the girls?'

'Didn't get out of the swimming pool in time and were disqualified for late entry.'

I made some kind of derogatory comment about form 2's lack of organisation just at the point when Matthew happened to be passing on his fifth visit to the lavatory. It was the kind of remark I should have kept to myself; it was exactly what Matthew had been waiting for. He spent the next half hour defending the dignity of his class, his chess club and his universe. By the time we got him into bed again I was ready to concede anything; anything as long as it ended in silence.

For the rest of the evening I got more than enough of silence. Matthew's stream of words seemed to have had the opposite effect on Sam who had become positively monosyllabic. He managed to show enthusiasm when we got involved in a conversation on the pros and cons of rhyme but I couldn't sustain my interest for long and was forced to lapse into silence.

It was a relief when the phone rang. I said a loud hello into the receiver. I got back a tiny greeting accompanied by background noises of drunken revelry.

'Hello,' I said again.

'Kate.' The small voice hadn't got any bolder, 'I'm scared. He was watching again tonight.'

'Alicia?' I asked. I heard a small sob which I took to be

assent. 'Where are you?'

The background noises sounded closer and now I heard banging, as if she'd dropped the phone. The voice that took over from hers was loud and slurred.

'She's in the swing,' the voice joked, 'not bad for a classical musician. She's seeing the world as it can be, and boy are we having fun. Aren't we, darling?'

The last word was strung out for cockney effect but the speaker didn't quite make it: he couldn't erase the rounded tone of his accent and he faltered as if he'd lost his way. His hesitation gave Alicia the time she needed. She must have grabbed the receiver back. When I heard her voice again it sounded slightly stronger.

'You will come tomorrow?' she asked. 'You have to.'

'I'll come now if you'd like me to,' I answered. 'Where are you?'

I didn't get an answer. Instead I was wished a happy Christmas by one voice and all the luck in the world by another. After that they left the phone to dangle. I hung on trying to pick up clues as to the venue but all I heard was the diffuse sound of rather desperate merry-making indulged in by either the very young or the very bored. By the sounds of the voices accompanying her, Alicia was moving in circles which included both. But that's as much as I gleaned before somebody hung up.

I waited a while in case she phoned again but nothing happened. I went to bed worrying about her and worrying about the fact that I hadn't even started the job and already I was feeling responsible. I wondered what it was about Alicia that made her seem, despite the outward trappings of wealth and confidence, so vulnerable.

Three

       I fell asleep worrying about it and I woke with Alicia on my mind. Matthew helped drive her out temporarily. Up at seven and roaring around the flat since five past, he was a changed person. Gone was the sulkiness, the persistent irritability of the night before, to be replaced by shining eyes and a thirst for conversation that knew no bounds.

'Amazing what ten hours' sleep will do,' I said to Sam.

He groaned and turned over. 'Don't I wish I could find out,' he muttered.

I left him to it, and went to join Matthew who was fuelling himself for the day by eating a cocktail of cereals from a variety pack, topped by overflowing milk. At least I think that's what he was having. I tried not to look too closely while I drank a cup of coffee.

Matthew kept up with the eating and the talking until Sam dragged himself out of bed and the two of them out of the door. I could hear the conversation, the high excited tones of Matthew and the grunted replies from Sam, as they made their way down the stairs and towards the car.

When their voices had tailed off, I got dressed. After that, I reckoned that the hour was now respectable to give the Weatherbys a ring.

I dialled without really thinking about it and so I was unprepared when Mrs Weatherby answered. I felt slightly foolish as I spoke.

'It's Kate Baeier,' I said. 'Could I speak to Alicia?'

There was a slight hesitation before she replied. She sounded tense.

'My daughter had a late night,' she said. 'I am loath to disturb her. Is it important?'

'Not really,' I heard myself replying, 'I just wanted to check that she got back all right.'

'I can assure you she did. I have trained her well.'

She sounded as if she was talking about some kind of performing seal but I didn't think it politic to tell her so.

'That's good,' I said. 'Could you tell her I'll see her tonight?'

'I'll pass the message on, Miss Baeier.'

I thanked her and was about to hang up when she spoke again. The words came out rushed but strong, nevertheless. 'Alicia is young and impressionable,' she said. 'As I am sure we all were at her age. And she can be prone to exaggeration. I wouldn't get too carried away if I were you.'

I made some assenting noises while I wondered what she was getting at. She ignored them. She hadn't finished with me yet.

'Alicia also has a way of appealing to people's protective instincts. I would be grateful if you could remember that she does have a mother and that she is still under-age.'

I said I'd bear it in mind and then hung up. Her goodbye sounded triumphant; mine was confused. Marion Weatherby was a tricky customer but her warning contained more than a grain of truth: I was becoming too involved with Alicia. I should never have rung to check up on her. My job was to find out who was following her and I resolved to stick to it.

There was no way Gordon Jarvis of Mately's was going to arouse my protective instincts. For a start he kept me waiting a full forty-five minutes and then, when I was ushered in, he gave a glance at his precision-balanced, over-sized Swiss watch to show me that the action had been deliberate. I could have told him that he needn't have bothered. Ever since I'd landed the contracts compliance work I'd been in a

21

unique position to study the use of time by the average English businessman. Jarvis's tactics were not unusual for a certain type of operator: by experience I'd learned that men like him showed a rather unimaginative approach to stalling and a tendency to try and get their own way by bullying. None of this did I tell Gordon Jarvis. Instead I returned his hearty handshake, sat down in the leather swivel chair to which I'd been pointed, and refused sugar in my coffee. I should also have refused the coffee, but how was I to know?

He threw me a long hard look which gave me the opportunity to examine him. He was a handsome man, if slightly on the garish side. A big frame had been kept in trim by constant surveillance if the way he looked at the two chocolate digestives in front of me was anything to go by. His suit was charcoal grey and tailored to fit his broad shoulders. His shirt was pink and pinstriped. He seemed ill at ease with the combination, as if he were trying to live out somebody else's idea of what he should be wearing. His watch and the gold chain that hugged his thick neck seemed more in character but I thought that whoever was dressing him would soon get rid of them.

I let my inspection go on a trifle too long which lost me some points in the game we were about to play. I tried to recoup them by crunching into a biscuit that I didn't feel like and was rewarded by the look of envy that crossed his face. He decided that his best bet was to get down to business.

'How can I help you, Kate?' he said. 'Don't mind if I call you that?'

'Well, Gordon,' I replied, 'my visit is by way of a routine check. As you know I'm authorised by the borough purchasing department to investigate its potential suppliers . . .'

'Suspicious lot, you reds,' Jarvis interrupted. I ignored him; I'd heard it too many times before.

'. . . and in particular on the company's policy on equal opportunities for women and ethnic minorities. I gather you were sent our questionnaire earlier in the month . . .'

22

'My secretary deals with details,' Jarvis said. 'I like to delegate. And that shows how much I trust my girls, which should please you lot.'

'. . . and we received it back recently.' I reached into my briefcase and brought it out. I made a pretence of reading what I'd already had plenty of time to study while waiting in Jarvis's ante-room.

'You do not seem to have anybody from the Bengali community in your employ,' I said.

Jarvis leaned back in his chair and leered at me.

'Why them?' he said. 'Are they flavour of the month at your place? You'd better watch it: two can play your game. I'll report you for discrimination against other dark skins.'

'Your factory is in Smithfield,' I said, 'where there is a large Bengali community. I'm surprised none has applied to work at Mately's.'

Jarvis had had enough of the game. He lumbered to his feet.

'I'm a self-made man,' he said, 'but I can't be everywhere at once. I have a personnel manager whom I pay well. He hires and fires. Ask him.'

He moved to the door, opened it and yelled 'Shirley!' to the woman who couldn't have been more than ten feet away. 'Give our visitor Mr Samson's number. And get Longford's on the phone. I've got a busy day ahead.'

We smiled at each other as he stood aside for me to pass. His smile was one of contempt. I felt an impulse to try and wipe it off but that passed as the door closed.

Shirley was blonde and painted and efficient. She'd dialled a number, switched it through and typed a letter of introduction for me before I reached her desk. She smiled at me perfunctorily. She too had a busy day in front of her. As I reached to take the letter from her I saw that she'd been occupied checking a long list of machinery.

'Ordering new stock?' I asked.

She nodded and her eyes strayed towards the papers from

which I'd distracted her. I followed her gaze.

'Unusual time of year for it, isn't it?' I asked. 'Trying to reduce your tax bill?'

'We had a fire,' she said. 'We're still catching up.'

I'd just been making conversation, seeing where it would lead me, and I was about to give up when Gordon Jarvis came bursting through the door. The look of genial amusement he'd displayed while seeing me was more than gone. His face was red with fury.

'Miss Baeier,' he yelled. 'I run a business here and I cannot tolerate your disturbing my staff. Kindly vacate the premises.'

I saw that the expression on Shirley's face mirrored my own look of surprise. This outburst was obviously not part of Jarvis's daily repertoire. It frightened even him. He dropped his voice.

'We are all working under pressure here,' he said. 'Let me show you out.'

He hustled me to the door and pushed me through it. Then he stood watching while I walked down the corridor.

I turned the corner and then I stopped. I waited until I heard the door closing. Then slowly I walked back. I stood outside their office and checked up and down the corridor. When I was sure that no one was in sight, I put my ear to the door.

He was still at it, and although the full force of his anger had abated, he wasn't letting her get away lightly. I couldn't make out the sentences but the occasional word, punctuated by what sounded like a fist hitting the desk, was loud enough to reach me. I heard him say something about confidentiality and loyalty and I heard him talk over her muted protests.

After a while his voice faded and I thought I heard his inner door shutting. The secretary's chair was pushed back and high heels clicked towards the door.

I backed away. I thought briefly about the layout of the place before running left down the corridor. I turned the corner and peered back towards her office. When she came out I knew that I had guessed correctly. She walked to the right, faltering but determined, until she reached the toilets. She went in. I followed.

I opened the door and hesitantly went inside. I needn't have bothered pausing. The place seemed completely empty and I was faced with an array of sludge-green doors which looked out on to grimy basins. One of the doors was shut. From behind it I could hear the soft sounds of her sobs mingling with the gurgling of water down a drain. I left her to it.

Everything I had read in Carmen's reports indicated that Gordon Jarvis was not strapped for cash. Mately's, the company he'd founded with a healthy injection of capital, was reckoned a promising newcomer, and if it could break into the educational market by starting with a large order from the ILEA, its future was secure. Even without the order, Jarvis was not about to go under.

Despite the fact that he seemed to have access to large cash reserves, Jarvis was prudent in his expenditure. His factory was in Smithfield, but his offices were rented from one of those concerns that divide warehouses into more units than should be physically possible. True, Jarvis had rented in the better part of the building – the top, which was more spacious and where the windows allowed some daylight to filter through – but the communal facilities had to be suffered by all. The toilets where I'd left Shirley were large and school-like. The cafeteria, which I found after many enquiries and wrong turns, wasn't much better. The management had attempted to jazz the place up by furnishing it with individual bottle-green table and chair affairs, some of which were incongruously topped by striped green umbrellas, but they couldn't disguise the smell of month-old stew and the sight of salad composed of wilted lettuce and half-dead tomatoes.

I settled for a pot of tea on the grounds that the coffee must be worse. If I was right, God help the coffee-drinkers. I kept a nervous eye on the door. I was relieved when Shirley came in alone.

She wasn't looking around her as she went to the counter. I watched as she chose a small side salad and a black coffee. She paid and turned to scan the tables. She couldn't have been concentrating because she missed me entirely. She walked up to an empty table. She put her tray down and sat. She placed the salad in front of her and began to toy with it dispiritedly.

I went up to her table and stood beside her. I pulled at a chair, until she looked up. I saw that her face had been freshly made up but the powder couldn't hide the anger in her eyes.

'May I?' I asked.

She didn't reply, so I sat down. 'He gave you a rough ride,' I said.

She shrugged as if she didn't care but her shoulders sagged just enough to show how much it mattered. Her lips curved downwards almost imperceptibly and beneath the cover of smoothly applied make-up I thought I caught a hint of lingering misery. She used her fork to spear the tomato and bring it towards her mouth. She grimaced as she saw what was heading her way and let her hand fall.

'Food's as bad as the job,' she said. 'I'll be well out of it.'

'You're leaving?' I asked.

She looked me directly in the face. Her anger was there, ready to leap out at the wrong word.

'I don't take that sort of treatment from anybody,' she said. 'A year I've worked for that man, and never put a foot wrong. I thought we had an understanding. Well I see we didn't and I've given my notice.'

'Why was he so angry?' I asked.

The anger that had lighted her face faded and was replaced by despondency. I guessed she was staring bleakly into a future of job-hunting and penny-pinching.

I tried to draw her back. 'When was the fire?'

'Eight, nine months ago,' she said. 'In the new factory. He

26

practically lost everything, but he was insured. His type always come out on top. Didn't affect him financially – don't know what he got into such a state about.'

'Maybe he's trying to hide something about it,' I said.

She looked at me again. She didn't like what she saw.

'Leave me alone,' she said. 'Haven't you caused enough trouble for one day? Bleeding do-gooders with your questionnaires.'

I rose. There didn't seem much point in staying. I reached into my briefcase and took out a card. I put it down in front of her. She didn't budge.

'In case you want to talk,' I said.

I walked away from her towards the exit. Then I turned back. She was sitting still and hunched over her food. She looked as if she would never move again, but my card had gone from the table.

Carmen was leaving the office on her way to lunch when I arrived. I joined her. We spent an hour eating pizza which had never seen a mozzarella cheese but was otherwise okay, and discussing our cases. I told her about my visit to Mately's and Carmen said she'd put out a few feelers to see whether anybody was gossiping about the causes of the fire. We agreed that, at least for formality's sake, I would go and see the personnel manager. In my experience personnel people always manage to combine a natural gregariousness with a closed mouth when it comes to company secrets. But we agreed it might be worth a try.

'Anyway, I think you could be right,' I said as we reached the limit of the Jarvis conversation. 'Something about that organisation feels fishy.'

Carmen pushed her sticky chocolate fudge slice away from her. She spoke in a voice full of despondency. 'I could be wrong. It was probably all my imagination.'

I looked at her in amazement.

'Imagination? You? The woman who once spent twenty minutes telling me that imagination was better left to those who could afford it?'

Carmen didn't smile.

'Yeah well,' she said, 'maybe financial security's getting to me. I'm losing my touch.'

There it was again: defeat in Carmen's voice.

'What brought this on?' I asked.

'The Weatherbys,' she said. 'I can't get anywhere on them. I can't trace the source of their wealth. Nor can I find any mention of Mr Weatherby. I've tried everything.'

'Perhaps their story is just not very interesting,' I said. 'Or they keep a low profile.'

Carmen shook her head.

'Thing about money is that it leaves a trail when it's in sufficient quantity. I'm losing my touch.'

I didn't take that comment too seriously. I'd learned a while ago that Carmen could combine the most supreme self-confidence with a low opinion of herself. I think it was caused by not having had a consistent work record. Somewhere at the back of her mind, she suspected that she would one day fall flat on her face and not be able to get up. When she'd first shown me the fear I'd tried to reason with it: I'd soon learned that it was non-negotiable. Sometimes I suspected that Carmen kept it lurking just so that she couldn't feel too good. That way life wouldn't surprise her, nor would it turn on her unexpectedly. I hadn't found a way to discuss it with her: when I tried I got a warning, and Carmen's warnings can be quite ferocious. So, usually, I left her alone and waited for her to come out of the mood.

That day I decided to have a go.

'Maybe you should trust your failure rather than doubting it,' I said.

'What do you mean?' Carmen snapped. 'You going growth movement-ish on me?'

'Would I ever?' I said. 'What I mean is, trust that if you can't find anything then either there really is nothing to find . . .' I held up my hand to stem the imminent protest, '. . . or they've hidden it for a reason. So go dig for the dirt.'

Carmen didn't reply and I didn't pursue it. I knew when I'd pushed my luck as far as it would go. We paid the bill and we parted. As I watched her walk off I thought I detected a spring in her step which hadn't been there before.

I was due at Alicia's concert that evening and so I decided to take the afternoon off. I spent a bit of time wandering around the shops in search of diversion. I didn't have much success. At one point I found myself standing stock still in front of a stall in Camden Passage staring into space. I was shaken out of my waking dream by the stallholder.

'Anything of interest?' she asked.

I shook my head.

'Move along then,' she suggested. 'Give the real customers a chance.'

I moved along.

Dalston looked the same as when I'd last left it – which, I realised, had been some time ago. Ever since Matthew's schedule with Sam had been changed, I'd been spending less and less time at my flat and more with the two of them grappling for the available space at Sam's. I betted Sam was pleased about that. He'd long ago started a campaign to get us to live together and it felt like he had taken a lesson from Mao's long march in carrying it out. He didn't often mention his wish but it was always there in the undertow waiting to pounce. Increasingly I wondered why I was hanging on to my lone retreat.

Not that day, though. I put a bunch of white freesias into a black vase, sat down on the sofa, put my feet up and revelled in my solitude. I loved my flat. I loved the quiet of it and the fact that it had been decorated without any of the compromises that came from sharing. Years of communal living had made my choice seem precious to me and I was loath to give up on it. I knew that some day soon the constant journeying from one base to another would get too much but at present I was still interested in having this as a bolt-hole. I lay still, enjoying the calm.

I woke up an hour later – tired, frazzled and disoriented. I ran myself a bath. I soaked in it while I sipped at a vodka and tonic. After that I fried myself a quick steak which I ate with an indifferent tomato salad and some crusty brown bread. I was ready to face the world. All I had to do was get dressed.

I thought about appropriate clothes for a minute but when I looked through my wardrobe I realised that the thinking had been purely theoretical. I knew I wouldn't be able to compete with Alicia's black number so I settled for semi-respectable and warm. I took a guess that St James's wouldn't have the kind of central heating that would encourage short sleeves.

One look at the mink coats arrayed round plump shoulders inside the church and I knew that I'd guessed right. I picked up my complimentary ticket from the boy at the desk, outstared his curious look and made for the central aisles.

I had to squeeze past a number of substantial knees on the way to my seat. Their owners, without exception, chose to ignore me as I climbed over them. I settled down to listen to the conversations which, though coming from different directions, all seemed to centre on the absolute fascination of Harry's projected hunt or Margaret's faux pas on the cricket field. The talk seemed so stereotyped that, initially, I thought that everybody in the hall was chanting to the same tune. But when I got acclimatised and had time to look around I realised that I had been given a seat among the older members of the audience. On the sides of the church sat the younger age-group – slightly less well-heeled and definitely less conventional. I wondered why Alicia had chosen to put me in the place that her mother should have occupied.

The musicians filed on at exactly eight p.m. – fourteen of them bustled to take their seats, laughing and talking as they did so, seemingly without nerves. They settled themselves down and tuned up, so that a whole array of long-held notes came out to us. They were dressed formally – dinner suits and long evening affairs – and they were all under twenty. Colours were restricted to black and white with the exception of one daring member at the back of the second row who had snuck a red silk shirt on top of her flowing black skirt. Alicia was not among them.

She didn't turn up for the first number. It was a rendering of Mozart's 30th which, boring at the best of times, never really got off the ground with this crew. There was applause when it ended but it was noticeably muted. I thought how hard this profession must be for the young; even with a sympathetic audience of friends and relatives, they were being judged.

We got a bit more scraping of bows after the first piece, as if they were trying to excuse the level of playing by a failure of tuning. I looked round the church, taking in the heights above us, the brown wood and fancy trimmings and the incongruously positioned television lights. I tried to concentrate on single men in the audience but, without a description, it was pretty hopeless.

I was still looking to the back when the hall went quiet. There was an expectant hush. I turned just in time to see the conductor walk back into the limelight. He received another smattering of polite applause and he smiled tightly as if he had expected more. But it was Alicia for whom the audience was waiting. That much was obvious when she came on. It wasn't that the applause was any louder but it was more concentrated, more spontaneous and more welcoming.

She smiled briefly towards us as she reached the central music stand. She and the conductor nodded to each other – a nod of greeting between two professionals. Then she tuned up quickly, quietly and efficiently. She, of all the kids there, looked nervous, wired up and ready to bolt. She held herself straight and tense. She stopped tuning and she nodded to the conductor again.

And then they began. As soon as they did, I understood the audience's expectation. Alicia played like a dream. She was leading on Mozart's 40th, the Jupiter, and she played it

31

for all it was worth. Colour sprang to her cheeks as she immersed herself in the music and, as if in response, the orchestra started to play together in a way they hadn't managed before.

I admit I was impressed. But I was also confused. Alicia seemed faultless. And yet I couldn't help feeling that some of the audience's admiration was a result of her appearance. Her dark eyes flashed and her body bent itself to the instrument. It was almost as if they were locked together. It was as if the music were part of her very being, so that it seemed to radiate back out at us. We were being included in something special; it was almost as if we were playing for her, willing her to get to the end.

I realised then why it was that I felt uneasy. It was the element of desperation in Alicia's playing. She was using that violin as if her life depended on it.

It felt very different from the time I'd heard her on the piano. Then her playing had been passionate and undisciplined, but the passion sprang from life. This time it spoke more of dread.

I don't think I was the only one who was affected by her performance. When the piece finished there was a stunned silence. It was a silence that could almost have been one of embarrassment. We had all been onlookers on somebody else's too intense pain.

Alicia didn't seem to have rejoined us yet. She stared straight ahead. I followed her gaze. I saw she was looking at a man in his late forties whose eyes were fixed on her.

Two things happened at once. The audience pulled itself out of its collective trance and began to clap. The applause sounded thunderous, coming as it did after so intense a silence. At the same time, Alicia gave a perfunctory bow and exited. Still grasping her violin she fled to the back of the hall. The man she'd been looking at got up and pushed his way after her. He moved surprisingly fast, given his bulk.

I tried to go after them quickly but I'd reckoned without the opposition. This time when I pushed past the people in my row, I got plenty of notice – most of it derogatory. It was a mark of just how affected the crowd had been by the performance: they needed some target to diffuse their tension and I was as good as anything.

I got out in one piece eventually. I was just in time to see the man going through the entrance doors, following a rapidly retreating Alicia. I made to go after him. And failed.

I found my path blocked by a young man. He stood in front of me and he made no attempt to make it seem like an accident. When I tried to manoeuvre round him he placed a restraining hand on my shoulder.

'Leave the lady alone,' he said.

'Aren't you picking on the wrong person?' I answered. 'I'm not the one who's been following her.'

The hand didn't move. The boy snorted. What came out was an imitation of a contemptuous laugh. I lifted my own arm and picked his off me. Then I looked him squarely in the face.

He must have been about nineteen and yet already he looked tired out by life. He had the sort of ineffectual features sported by public school products, but his were jaded and spoiled. Dark rings lined his weak blue eyes. A vague stubble around his chin made him look more unkempt than menacing. His mouse-brown hair was a shade too long for its fashionable cut and a shade too dirty for me.

He backed away from my scrutiny.

'Alicia doesn't need you,' he said. 'I'll look after her.'

I recognised the voice.

'Like you were looking after her last night,' I said. 'When she phoned.'

His peaky face flushed. 'That was a joke. I was drunk and so was she.'

'She sounded scared to me,' I replied.

Again the boy experimented with a laugh. 'You don't know Alicia like I do,' he said, 'or her family. Don't think you can come in and save the day. I'm warning you, I'll look after her.'

There was something about the way he was talking that had been puzzling me: something about the flatness of his voice and the implied menace in his stance. I looked at his eyes more closely and noticed how they bulged. I reached forward and grabbed at him.

He was taken by surprise and didn't have time to move out of the way. I had pulled up the sleeve of his dingy white shirt before he realised what I was aiming for. We both looked at the track marks near his veins and at the punctures on his hands.

'Doesn't seem to me that you're in such great shape to look after yourself,' I said, 'never mind Alicia.'

I couldn't tell whether the flush that came to his face was provoked by anger or by shame. It didn't stay there long enough. Instead it was replaced by that look of artificial calm that junkies learn to perfect. He rolled his sleeve back down again.

'Alicia knows what I am,' he said. 'It's me she chose. You know nothing.'

'I know Alicia's in trouble,' I said. 'I want to help.'

The boy hesitated for a fraction of a second. I watched while conflicting emotions crossed his face. I thought he was deciding something – deciding whether to trust or discard me.

I thought he was about to make up his mind in my favour when we were interrupted. Alicia came back into the entrance hall. She was alone. Her cheeks were tear-stained but otherwise she looked unharmed.

The boy broke away from my gaze and went up to her. He took her in his arms, and his hands stroked the back of her neck. It was done with an extraordinary tenderness: the kind you don't often see, especially in public.

She rested with him for a moment. She was completely still. She had the look of a hunted animal which had found a temporary refuge. But she wasn't properly relaxed. It was as if she knew that the hunt would soon resume.

When she saw me, she broke away from the embrace. 'Did

34

you enjoy the music?' she asked me.

'I felt it,' I said. 'Very strongly.'

'Yes, that happens sometimes,' she said blithely. Her face had hardened. The fear was now covered by a mask of teenage politeness.

'Was that the man?' I asked.

The politeness didn't budge. Instead she added a touch of superciliousness to it.

'What man?' she asked.

'The one who followed you out. Is he the man who's been scaring you?'

'I don't know who you're talking about,' she stuttered, 'I felt faint after my performance and went out to get some air. I saw no man.'

I opened my mouth to say something but was interrupted. Two ushers flung the doors between the hall and the church open. The sound of diminishing applause greeted my ears and was quickly followed by the advance guard of an audience which seemed relieved to have been let off the hook.

The young crowd was out first. Alicia used the fact to her advantage. She greeted a sombre couple as if they were lifesavers in a social gaffe. They looked slightly surprised but were ready to play along with her. Soon the three of them were chatting animatedly. The boy with Alicia stood to one side, guarding them.

The group soon grew in size. Alicia knew how to attract attention, that much was obvious. She stood in the centre of a vivacious crowd, spinning a conversation of triviality around herself. She acted like she had not a care in the world, like she was just another teenager caught up in a bustling social whirl. I wondered how her boyfriend felt about it. He stood his ground but there was no doubt that he was isolated. His posture expressed the fact that, without his attachment to Alicia, this was the last place he would have chosen to be.

The distaste he displayed was mutual. I saw a number of

35

the youths raise their eyebrows at his presence and one or two deliberately snub him. He ignored them.

The group chattered wildly while the adult members of the audience filed past. I could distinguish individual voices as they tried to work out what they should all do. Alicia's suggestions were numerous. It sounded as if the last thing she wanted to do was to go home and she was doing her best to prevent anybody else proposing it.

They finally decided on Amy's, a club in Piccadilly. They took a long time about it but eventually they began to move off. For a second, Alicia detached herself from the gang.

'You can go home,' she told me. 'I shan't be needing you again tonight.'

With that she quickly rejoined her friends, deliberately surrounding herself with their high spirits.

I was astonished. That was the third Alicia who had been revealed to me: the small child in front of her mother, the woman wrapped in her music and the spoilt brat at home with the rich. I wondered which one was the real Alicia. I was still wondering when the thing I least expected occurred: I was picked up.

He was ten years younger than me but he didn't know that. Or maybe he'd decided to go for the older woman. Whatever his reasons, he moved in on me.

'All on your own?' he asked.

I nodded and looked at him. He was quite a pleasant sight in an undistinguished kind of way. He was dressed in one of those baggy suits which can drown the unconfident and he just about managed to carry it off. His deep brown hair was slicked back so that his face stood out. It was a nice face, clear-skinned and smooth, and what it lacked in depth it made up for in charm. All in all, he wasn't bad-looking, and maybe the years would add some interest.

I don't know what he made of my scrutiny; he certainly didn't hide from it. Instead, he bore it patiently and when I'd finished he tossed me a dazzler of a smile. He thrust his right hand towards me.

'Name's Toby Stafford,' he said.

I told him my name and we shook on it. I was at a loss as to how to behave — it had been at least fifteen years since anybody had tried to pick me up like this and I wasn't quite sure of the etiquette. He didn't seem to mind: I guessed he must operate in a world where boys still think that it is their right and duty to make the running.

'How about coming for a drink?' he asked.

It was on the tip of my tongue to call an end to this charade but then I had second thoughts.

'I'm game if we can go to Amy's,' I said.

A flash of disappointment crossed his face. 'You don't want to stick it out with that crowd? What about somewhere quieter?'

'I'm in the crowded mood,' I said.

He gave in gracefully if transparently. I could almost hear his thoughts as he transferred his fantasy from a candlelight dinner for two, to an entrance with strange and new woman. It didn't quite have the same appeal for him but he could go with it.

He just had to drive the two hundred yards in his Maserati. That meant we had to find another parking space and it took us some time to reach the door of Amy's. When we did, he insisted on paying for me. I, who believed that these old-fashioned habits were well and truly dead, was oddly touched. One thing was sure: this was going to be a night to remember.

The place was packed out and pulsating. It was filled with what I suppose could be described as the young set, all drinking champagne as if Armageddon awaited. Their formal evening attire contrasted strangely with their unruly behaviour which seemed to be full of sexual innuendo combined with hysterical horseplay.

My escort steered me past black marble tables surrounded by cavorting guests to a corner. He must have had some influence in the place because when we arrived, a table was miraculously waiting for us. He made sure I was seated and then he sat beside me.

He'd guessed my response to the place accurately enough.

'Somewhere quieter would have been much more conducive,' he whispered in my ear, thus enabling himself to come even closer. 'Are you sure you wouldn't rather go elsewhere?'

'It's an education,' I said. 'I'm always ready for new experiences.'

'Me too,' he replied softly.

This was getting out of hand. It looked as if my inexperience was showing and that he'd carry on out-manoeuvring me. I tried to hide my discomfort but I'm sure he guessed it. He smiled sardonically before waving for a waitress.

He got her attention immediately and he ordered for us. When I asked for white wine he steered away from the champagne option and instead showed a thorough and learned knowledge of the vintage list. When the wine arrived he offered me the first taste of it and smiled when I approved. When it came to seduction technique I could see he wasn't a novice.

I had been searching the boisterous crowd for Alicia and suddenly I spotted her. She was sitting at a table, her sullen boyfriend in attendance but slightly pulled back from her, surrounded by the laughing gang. She looked feverish; over-involved in excitement which bordered on tears.

My companion saw me looking and moved closer to distract me. He might have succeeded except at that point we were interrupted. With a shout of 'Toby, darling!' a nineteen-year-old with big teeth and curly hair screeched to a halt at our table. Toby darling introduced me to Patricia love, and her friend Richard. Richard did not seem to come with an endearment but they made up for this by stressing the second rather than first syllable of his name.

The two of them sat down beside us with a smoothness that had to be admired. They were soon tucking into the vintage with abandon.

Patricia didn't like the look of me – that much was clear. So she set about being utterly charming. She was one of those women who have been brought up to compete with others for male attention and who, inside, hate themselves for doing it. Every smile she shot me was an arrow aimed at puncturing my self-confidence and bolstering her own prestige. I wondered whether the fondness that she and Toby displayed didn't hide some past hurt between them.

'Can't say I've seen you here before,' she said to me.

'My first time,' I said.

'Lucky you,' she answered. She gave me a second look, assessing the degree of my ability to survive her jibe.

'I went to the concert at St James's,' I said, 'to hear Alicia Weatherby play.'

'Didn't everybody, darling,' Patricia brayed 'So talented is Alicia. Pity about Pete.'

'Her companion?' I asked.

'If one could call him that. Not that I understand how he could keep anybody company. I always thought Alicia must have a very sleazy side to her.'

'Now, now, Patricia, let's not be bitchy,' Richard said in a voice that called for further excesses.

'Honestly, though,' she said, picking up her cue, 'what does she see in him? All that dreadful lamenting about life. I mean, we all have problems but we have to make the best of what we've got. Enjoy it while you can, that's what I say.'

'You can't take it with you,' Richard contributed.

'Life is too short,' Patricia intoned.

It was my turn. 'And one swallow doesn't make a spring,' I contributed.

I got confused looks from the two newest additions to the table and an admiring smile from Toby.

'What's Pete's problem?' I asked.

'Talent,' Patricia said.

'Or the lack of it,' Richard said.

'Quite,' Patricia added.

'In which department?' I asked.

39

'Why, music, of course,' Richard said. 'That's what we're all interested in, isn't it?'

'And Peter just didn't have the staying power,' Patricia said, 'so he tried to blame it on lack of opportunity. Making those ridiculous fusses about how he never had access to a first-rate teacher or a good violin. And it's not even as if Pete is poor. He practically oozes money these days. But that doesn't stop him moaning. My dear, it's such a bore. We all know that he simply was not good enough. Those that are rise to the top.'

'Like flotsam,' I said.

Patricia and Richard exchanged a look that might have led to other things if I hadn't seen Alicia get up. I craned my neck to see where she was going and noticed that Pete had followed her. I kept my eyes on the two of them.

They walked my way. When they got to our table Alicia stopped. She ignored my companions and spoke directly to me.

'I'm going home now, Kate,' she said. 'Honestly I am. You've no reason to worry. I'm sorry about my behaviour. I'll see you tomorrow.'

I asked if I could come a bit earlier and talk to her and she agreed. I watched as she walked out.

Their visit had broken the mood at our table. I tried to get more information from my companions.

'What about Pete and drugs?' I asked.

'Oh everybody takes drugs nowadays,' Patricia said. I looked at her bright eyes and clear skin and wondered whether she knew that she was talking from ignorance. She didn't catch my look. Instead, bored with me and my questions, she was idly scanning the room. She saw someone in the distance and she waved wildly.

'There's Susannah,' she said excitedly to Richard. 'Do let's join her.'

They got up and were gone as quickly as they'd arrived.

My companion gave a sigh of relief.

'Sorry about that,' he said, 'it always happens here.

Wouldn't you rather go somewhere quieter?'

'I would,' I said, 'but I'm afraid where I want to go is home.'

A look of expectation flared in his face.

'Alone,' I said.

He dealt with it well. He rose, and placed a few bills on the table.

'I'll help you find a taxi,' he said.

He was as good as his word. The perfect gentleman, he stood with me until a taxi arrived and I had told it where to go. Only when I was inside did he try again.

'We could have been good together,' he said.

'Maybe,' I answered, 'in another time, another place, another . . .'

'Don't say generation,' he said. 'You're not that old.'

He shut the door and the taxi drove off.

Sam was asleep in my bed when I got back. He rolled over and opened one eye as I climbed in.

'Where've you been?' he mumbled.

'Got picked up by a young man,' I answered.

'Lucky you,' he said and rolled back to his dreams.

Four

I was woken by a ring on the door. I dragged myself out of bed and to the intercom.

'Yes?' I shouted.

'Flowers,' a cheerful voice sang.

I pressed the buzzer and went downstairs. I took the bouquet from a cheery-looking delivery boy and dragged myself back upstairs. I removed the cellophane and smiled at the dozen red roses and at the accompanying card.

'For what might have been,' it said. Under the message was a telephone number.

Sam came out of the bedroom. 'They're nice,' he said.

'Mmm.'

'Secret admirer?' he asked.

'Last night's. I told you.'

'That's nice,' he repeated as he ambled to the bathroom.

Carmen was a thousand times more alert than Sam.

'You're early,' I said.

She smiled. 'Kaya and I went swimming this morning. And now I'm bursting with energy.'

'Funny. Exercise never had that effect on me,' I said. 'And I didn't know you ever indulged.'

Carmen smiled again. She didn't say anything. I looked more closely at her. Her face was relaxed, her skin was clear, her eyes were shining – all in all she was glowing. I'd often been forced to listen to exercise freaks expounding on the benefits of keeping fit, but Carmen seemed to be feeling the effects a trifle too soon. I wondered whether she was experiencing something other than a post-swimming glow.

'You're acting mighty funny these days,' I commented. 'What's up?'

'Nothing, girl,' Carmen replied, a broad grin now in evidence. 'On the contrary.'

'I see.' That was a lie: I thought I saw but maybe I was wrong. Maybe my brush with teenage sexuality was just making me more imaginative than usual.

She chose to put an end to my speculation.

'Listen to this,' she said. 'I saved it because I couldn't make it out.'

She flicked the switch on the answerphone and turned up the volume.

A man's voice boomed out. 'Great times . . .' Carmen cut him short. Abruptly she pushed buttons so that the tape whirled backwards. Her lips twitched.

So I was right! 'Mr Nothing I presume,' I said. 'Lucky you don't blush.'

Carmen didn't reply. She concentrated on finding the right place.

'Here it is,' she said.

This time we heard a woman's voice. There was a prolonged pause as she gathered up the courage to speak and when she did her voice came out halting and unsure.

'It wasn't right,' she said. 'I know I'm not supposed to be doing this, but it wasn't right.' There was another pause before she spoke again. 'Ask about Elmore,' she said. 'Talk to him.'

There was a ping as the machine registered her hanging up. I reached to switch it off but Carmen shook her head. 'There's more,' she said.

Sure enough, after two hangups which the machine registered as bleeps, the woman was back on the line. Her voice was stronger but it still gave nothing away.

'I don't want no more to do with it,' she said. 'Leave me alone from now on. Find Elmore.'

That was it. Carmen switched off the machine.

'Mean anything to you?' she asked. 'I've drawn a blank.'

I frowned. 'Let me hear it again.'

Carmen put it on again and this time I concentrated on the voice rather than the message. By the second call, I'd got it.

'That's Shirley,' I said. 'Jarvis's secretary. It's her voice.'

'Who's Elmore?' Carmen asked.

'Search me,' I said.

'Well, I've made you an appointment with Arnold Samson.'

I looked at her blankly.

'Jarvis's personnel manager,' she said.

'Oh goody,' I said.

She ignored that. 'Twelve-thirty,' she said. She handed me a piece of paper with an address written on it. I put it in my bag.

'I also looked into the Mately fire,' Carmen said. 'Nobody's talking about insurance fiddles. Word is that Jarvis didn't quite come out even from the damage – his cover wasn't good enough. He didn't lose much but equally he doesn't seem to have benefitted. His business is just secure enough to survive the jolt – if he can get that ILEA contract.'

I nodded my thanks at Carmen who was settling down at her desk. As I did so I spotted a pile of magazines she'd stacked there. I was surprised.

'What's with the *Harpers & Queens*?' I asked.

Carmen picked up the top copy and began thumbing through it. 'Just an idea,' she said.

She wasn't any more forthcoming than that so I turned to my paperwork. It was pretty tedious, but by noon I'd paid all the really outstanding bills and just about written enough invoices to ensure that, if they were paid promptly, my cheques would be honoured.

As I climbed the stairs to Arnold Samson's office I reflected on the fact that I was no longer sure where British capitalism

44

was headed. By all accounts Mately's was a going concern and yet there was a feeling of impermanence about it that would once have suggested poverty. The factory was at one location, the managing director at another and personnel manager at a third. But I knew that poverty hadn't created such decentralisation – instead it was a result of a fashionable kind of cost-cutting that said that geographical integrity was no longer relevant.

Arnold Samson looked as if he was grappling with worrying problems. A small, balding, harassed man, he had rolled up his white shirt sleeves to deal with encroaching paperwork and ringing telephones. He was sorting through the former and talking into the latter when I entered. He greeted me by waving a hand in the general direction of a badly stuffed chair which stood in front of his desk. Still talking with the receiver crooked to his ear he lit an Embassy Extra Mild by sliding a match against a glass paper weight. He drew on it heavily. He pushed the packet towards me and grimaced in sympathy when I shook my head.

He was coming to the end of his call. 'Try, if only as a favour to me, George,' he said and followed up by a series of rising 'uh, uhs' which reached a crescendo before turning into a brisk goodbye. He put the phone down with an air of satisfaction.

'What can I do for you?' he asked.

'Kate Baeier,' I said, 'About Mately's bid for the borough contract.'

'Ah yes,' he said. 'Coffee? Or something stronger?'

I settled for coffee and he bawled for his secretary to fetch it. It came in a chipped off-white mug and turned out to be a thick black brew. I wondered how anything could possibly be stronger.

Arnold drank his down with the speed of a true caffeine addict. In one smooth movement he emptied his overflowing ashtray into an equally overflowing bin beside him and he lit another cigarette. He grimaced again.

'I quite agree. Filthy habit,' he said. 'Must stop. Now, how

45

can I help?'

I repeated myself and he nodded furiously. He rose, hitched up his brown Terylene trousers so that they covered his bulging stomach and went up to a great four-drawer filing cabinet. There he occupied himself by pulling out files and muttering about systems. Finally he found what he was looking for. With a grunt of satisfaction he held up a sheaf of papers.

'Here we are,' he said triumphantly, 'never lost one of these yet.'

He took the papers back to his desk and rifled through them. When he'd finished he looked up at me.

'We filled in your questionnaire,' he said, 'what more can I do for you?'

'I'd be interested in a list of Mately's employees,' I said.

Samson frowned. It was something he should have trained himself out of: the effort created a series of furrows across his forehead which, with no hair to stop them, spread on to the top of his skull.

'Is this usual?' he said.

'You have an objection?' I asked innocently.

He looked me full in the face, taking my measure. Then he smiled.

'Well,' he said, 'can't see what harm it could do. Hold on half a mo.'

He left the room taking the papers with him. While he was gone I glanced idly round the place. It wasn't impressive. The furniture had seen better days, the windowsills could have been cleaner, the carpet had so many holes that it looked as if it had been attacked by some sort of killer moth. I got up and walked over to the filing cabinet.

Each drawer was separately labelled. Mately's was the name on the bottom one – the one where Samson had found his papers. The other drawers all bore different names.

I was pondering again on the subject of British capitalism – on what it meant when even the personnel directors were hired on a freelance basis – when I felt his breath on my neck. I didn't turn because I knew I would bump straight into his flab and I thought I'd like to live without that.

'Curious, aren't we?' he said. His voice was rigid with anger. He leaned across me and viciously pushed the Mately drawer closed. Then he stood a pace back so that I could get past him.

I sat down again. He handed me some sheets of paper clipped together. They had been photocopied on one of those machines that always takes two minutes longer to dry than you expect it to. I glanced through the lists of names as Samson stared at me broodingly from across his desk. It was a messy list, criss-crossed with deletions and white-outs but it was readable. When I'd finished I looked up.

'No Elmore,' I said.

This time the frown that crossed his face was more menacing. He kept his lips tightly sealed until he'd had time to think of a reply.

'Should there be?' he asked.

'You tell me,' I said.

He'd recovered his balance by now. He shot me a sleazy smile.

'Don't tell me the borough is going to force us to choose our employees by their names?' he said.

'I was told you employed an Elmore,' I said.

'You were misinformed, Ms Baeier,' he said. He stood up and reached across his desk, his palm upwards. I gathered he wanted his list back. I nearly asked him why he'd bothered to photocopy it if he was getting it back but, since I thought I knew the answer, there seemed no point.

I handed it to him and said goodbye. He nodded. He sat down. He was looking back at his desk when I left.

I left his office and headed for the nearest pay-phone. I dialled my work number. Carmen answered brightly.

'It's Kate,' I said. 'I need you to run some interference for me.'

I told her what had happened and what I wanted. She

agreed to set something up and be with me shortly. I said I'd meet her at the pub I'd noticed on my way in and then I went for lunch.

Carmen arrived within twenty minutes. She was not alone. She was accompanied by a tall man who looked at least ten years her junior. She introduced me to him, avoiding my questioning look. He shook my hand firmly and gave me a wide grin that acknowledged my interest.

Carmen took it upon herself to focus on the business in hand. 'So what's the routine?' she asked briskly.

'Fire alarm, I think. There's one on each floor.'

'And if they lock their offices?'

'No problem,' her friend interjected.

I showed them back to Samson's floor. The fire alarm, one of those cute red-boxed types with a dinky axe beside it, was located right outside Samson's office. For that reason I secreted myself in the nearest toilet while Carmen and friend dealt with the bell.

They didn't take long. Within one minute a loud clanging vibrated in the air. I heard a curse from the cubicle beside me and then the sound of the toilet flushing. The door was opened but I didn't hear the expected retreating clack of footsteps. Instead somebody rattled at my door.

'Are you deaf?' a woman's voice shouted. 'Fire!'

My heart sank. I recognised that voice. It belonged to Samson's secretary and the odds were that, if I could recognise her, then she would have no problem with me.

I tried to speak into my chest. 'I'll be out in a sec,' I said 'Go on without me.'

A hint of doubt crept into her voice. 'Well, if you're sure?'

'I'm fine. Just a bit occupied.'

She laughed. 'I know the feeling,' she said and then, to my relief, I heard her leave.

I gave her a few minutes' lead and then I stepped outside. The corridor was deserted. I looked through a window that led to a courtyard outside. I saw a crowd of people gathered together in groups of three and four chatting excitedly. There was a kind of carnival air about them, a kind of school's-out gaiety.

When I arrived at Samson's office Carmen's friend was at work on the lock. He smiled briefly at me.

'Any problems?'

'Easy,' he said and, with that, the door swung open. He stayed outside to mount guard; Carmen and I ran in. We got to the inner office fast and began rifling through the cabinets.

It didn't take me long to find what I was looking for. There, under 'Employees', was the list – the undoctored version. I scanned it hurriedly. And sure enough I found an Elmore. An Elmore James. I took down his address and then quickly replaced the paper and closed the cabinet.

There was no time to do anything else. A sharp knock on the exterior door warned us that already people were returning. Carmen and I ran out and the three of us took off down the corridor. Someone who had just climbed the stairs caught sight of us.

'Hey, you!' he yelled.

We ran off.

We went and had a celebratory drink in the dingy pub round the corner. In contrast to the greyness around us, we made a raucous crew, reliving other past victories. We talked of the time when we believed we could change the world, when everything seemed possible. It was an experience we had in common, despite the fact that they had been in England, while I was still living in Portugal. The memories of the fun we had once enjoyed came flooding back. We laughed, and our laughter fed itself until the tears were streaming down our faces.

'It's not like that any more,' Carmen said as the edge of laughter left her voice. 'It's serious now. There's ammunition on the street and it's not in our hands.'

'And the victories are work-related,' I said.

'Triumph of the self-employed, that's what we achieved

today,' Carmen's friend chipped in. I was impressed. The man was young but he wasn't naive.

This time he didn't seem to notice my scrutiny. He smiled and got up. He shook my hand. He nodded at Carmen, a slow intimate nod. She didn't acknowledge it.

'I'm on my way,' he said.

'Thanks for your help,' I said.

'Any time.' He nodded at Carmen again, and was off.

I drank the last of my lager. 'He seemed nice.'

Carmen got up. 'Let's get back to the office,' she said. 'I've got something to show you.'

With Carmen, explanation comes to those who wait. When we arrived back she went to her desk. She took a copy of *Harpers* that she had separated from the rest and opened it. She rifled through it until she got to the back and then she silently handed me a double-page spread of photographs. Her hand pointed to one in the left-hand corner.

I found myself looking at 'Jennifer's Diary' from six months previously. The page contained the usual array of social occasions with the usual selection of hearty-looking couples baring their teeth at each other in what passed for enthusiastic enjoyment. Each picture showed a different set but they all resembled each other so closely that it was some time before I could concentrate on the photo that Carmen had selected. When I saw it, I did a double-take.

'Gordon Jarvis,' I said.

'And look who he's with,' Carmen said, pride in her voice.

She had good reason to feel proud. There was a woman standing next to Jarvis, a woman who at first looked familiar only because she was so much of a type – a blonde, well-preserved, upper-class type. She was partially obscured by the fact that she was in the middle of toasting someone and she held her hand up in a way that covered her face. I thought I knew who she was, but before I got too excited I read the caption.

'Mrs Richard Weatherby, honorary secretary of the

Preservation Society, with Mr Gordon Jarvis, this year's man of the year.'

I looked at Carmen in admiration.

'How do you do it?' I asked.

'Desperation,' she said. 'I drew a blank on Marion Weatherby no matter where I turned so I decided to see whether she ever came out into the light. And for her type, where there's light, there's a camera with a flash on the end of it.'

I looked at the caption again. 'Mrs Richard Weatherby,' I said. 'Where's he?'

'No Richard,' Carmen replied. 'I got the girl I know who files for the Preservation Society to dig through the collective memory of the staff.'

'A girl you know at the Preservation Society?' I said. 'My, Carmen, you're getting more and more unpredictable.'

'Richard Weatherby hasn't been around for years,' Carmen continued after throwing me a dirty look. 'Nobody knows whether he's alive or dead. Marion Weatherby acts as if she'd rather be on her own. She has a series of men who accompany her to functions, Gordon Jarvis being the most recent, but she usually trades them in before it can become too serious. Jarvis is different. For a start he's not from the right mould – too self-made – but he's lasted longer than the rest. She even stuck her neck out to persuade the committee to award him this upper-class environmental award. She ran across a lot of opposition on the way but she sounds like more than a match for them. Once she wants something she gets it, according to my source.'

'The Jarvis connection can't be a coincidence,' I said. 'What has all this got to do with Alicia?'

'Maybe nothing,' Carmen suggested. 'Maybe Jarvis is up to something really dirty and he got his lady friend to hire you on a bogus investigation so that he can keep an eye on you.'

'I suppose it's possible . . .' I started and then I shook my head. 'No – can't be. Alicia is definitely in trouble. And there *is* a man following her. I don't get it: I don't get it at all.'

'You better go ask Elmore,' Carmen said.

Elmore James lived south of the river in one of those areas of London which don't really know what they're supposed to be. It was near Brixton but it didn't have the same energy: it was en route to Clapham but it didn't have the same look of up and coming opulence. Instead, it looked stranded and grey. Undistinguished houses were dwarfed by unsuccessful council estates and surrounded by roads which didn't seem to have anywhere much to go.

The address I'd taken from the Mately files led me to one of the most run-down of the houses. It was a poky, two-storey affair with peeling paint and neglected front yard. I rang the bell and, when that didn't yield any result, knocked on the door.

From inside the house I could hear the sound of loud reggae. The bass line beat against the walls of the house which seemed to be shaking in response. I knocked again. This time the music stopped.

I waited for what seemed an age. From inside the house came a kind of shuffling, as if somebody was hauling themselves along the corridor to the door. A chain rattled against the doorframe and then it opened up a crack. A face peered out.

'Yeah?' he said in a voice that couldn't have been less interested.

I could just about make out his features. He had a small face that had been scarred by stress: his brown skin was tinged with a grey that had nothing to do with age. I reckoned he must have been in his late teens but life had served him ill and the wariness in his eyes made him seem prematurely old.

'Yeah?' he said again.

'Elmore James?' I asked.

'Who wants to know?' he said.

'My name's Kate Baeier. I'd like to talk to you a minute.'

'What about?' he asked.

'Mately's,' I said.

I was semi-prepared for it so when he moved I was able to block him. As his hand pushed the door, I stuck my foot in the gap. He didn't have much force in his arms and I got a slow jarring feeling on my foot but nothing worse.

'I don't want to talk to you,' he said. 'Not about nothing. Ever.'

'I'm not from Mately's. I just want to know what you have on them.'

'Who says I'm connected?' he asked.

'You were employed there until recently. You left suddenly. Were you sacked?'

'Ask them.'

'They won't talk about you,' I said. 'What happened?'

He stared at me with what was very close to hatred. He was making a decision. When he finally made it, it came as a complete surprise. He undid the chain and flung the door open.

'What could have happened?' he yelled. 'Look at me!'

One look was enough to understand the grey pallor in his face and the shuffling towards the door. Elmore was in bad shape and he looked as if he'd recently been in worse. His body, held erect as if by force of will, was clothed in tattered jeans and a T-shirt, frayed enough to reveal grimy bandages underneath. The hand he held towards me showed the signs of recent scars. He shook as he held it in front of me, accusingly.

'I've suffered enough,' he shouted. 'Leave me alone.'

The force of the crippled hand had propelled me backwards. It gave him the opportunity he needed. Before I knew what he was doing he'd slammed the door in my face. I heard the bolt sliding back into place.

'Leave me alone,' he repeated, before he shuffled painfully away.

There was nothing I could do. I left him.

Carmen listened in silence to my story. She had a look on her face that I couldn't quite interpret.

'So you want me to have a try,' was all she said when I finished.

It wasn't a question, it was a statement, a recognition of where I was leading. I nodded.

'I don't like it,' she said.

'But you'll do it.' I finished the sentence as I had expected her to.

'Don't be so sure,' she said. There was a hint of finality in her voice and a touch of anger. It made me insecure.

'But you've always come through before,' I said. 'What's holding you back now?'

Carmen looked at me as if the question saddened her. 'I thought you might know,' she said softly.

'Oh shit, Carmen,' I said. 'You're talking in riddles. Is it your love life affecting you?'

I realised that it was an inappropriate thing to say as soon as I uttered it. In the back of my mind I did know what she was talking about. I just didn't want to face it.

I was on the point of apologising when Carmen stood up. 'That's not fair,' she said. She began to talk slowly, explaining herself as if I was an idiot. 'You want me to see Elmore because we're both black. My private life has nothing to do with it. It's your conscience that made you bring my friend into it.'

She was right – I did think that because of her skin colour Elmore would be more willing to talk. And that bothered me. I looked down at my hands. I didn't know what to say. I didn't like being caught out this way. It wasn't that there was anything wrong in the request *per se*. What Carmen didn't like was that I hadn't come out with it straight and she was right to be cross about it.

'I'm sorry,' I said weakly.

Carmen grimaced. She looked as if she was disappointed in me.

'You're the boss,' she said. 'I'll do it.'

'I wouldn't force you,' I said.

'It's too personal,' she said. 'Too much pain for too little reason. And now I'm getting enmeshed.'

'It's up to you,' I said again.

'And I said I'd do it,' she shouted. 'Just don't try and salve your conscience by making me tell you it's fine and dandy and it's what I always wanted.'

I nodded in answer. I felt sad – sad at the conversation and sad that I'd always known something like this would come up one day. However we tried to cut it, there was an inequality in power between us at work which increased with a built-in advantage that my colour bestowed on me. We could live with that, we could try and alter it, but we could never do so unless we remained honest with each other and with ourselves. I had just failed to be that honest.

I decided against putting what I was thinking into words. Just as I'd always known that something like this was bound to happen, so must Carmen have been waiting for it. Words, especially words aimed at diffusing the situation, wouldn't be any help. It was actions that counted.

I made us both a cup of coffee. 'Find out what he's got on Mately's,' I said. 'Or what they've got on him.'

Carmen nodded her consent at me. And then we both busied ourselves with other things.

Five

I arrived at Alicia's school in good time to meet her before the start of the concert. I'd reckoned without the school porter, the layout of the place and Alicia herself.

The school porter was the first obstacle. He hailed me as I tried to pass his glass cubicle in the entrance hall.

'Where ya going?' he shouted.

I looked round in case he was shouting at somebody else. There was no one in sight.

'I've come for the concert,' I said.

'Ave you now?' he sneered. 'Bit early aren't we?'

'There's somebody I want to see,' I said.

'There would be, wouldn't there,' he said, 'but you and me both know the rules. No entry after hours and you should have done your seeing before four o'clock.'

It took a while for his meaning to sink in. When it did, I was flabbergasted.

'I'm thirty-three,' I said.

'Yeah. And I'm your dead mum's auntie,' he said. 'Now clear out.'

Deadlock. I thought about pulling out my driving licence but the way he was heading towards me I didn't think I had the time. In fact, the way he was heading towards me, I didn't think I'd have time for anything. I backed towards the entrance.

And was saved from above.

'Mr Tolman,' an imperious voice called from the stairway, 'what are you doing?'

The caretaker smiled ingratiatingly. 'You know the rules ma'am,' he said. 'After all the vandalism: no pupils outside school hours.'

'Really, Mr Tolman,' the voice answered. 'This young woman is not one of ours. Surely you can see that?'

I smiled at my rescuer as she walked over to stand by me. She was the type of headteacher who, when I was fourteen, could have reduced me to a kind of emotional rubble. I was sure that, should she want to, she would be able to do so now.

She was dressed in a timeless fashion – good quality brown tweed skirt and tailored jacket to match, with a well-cut cream silk shirt. She was the sort of person who never had any doubt that her vision of the important virtues and the stability of the social fabric in Britain would win out. My encounter with the porter might illustrate how even the fanciest of schools had been affected by youth discontent, but this headteacher was still managing to hold back the tide of rebellion.

'You are looking for?' she asked.

'Alicia Weatherby,' I said.

'Ah, Alicia, so talented. We are indeed proud of her progress. Take the east wing staircase . . .'

Her instructions went on for a good two minutes. When she got to the end she repeated them just to make sure. I concentrated hard – she had that effect on people. By the time she'd finished I was practically hypnotised by the certainty in her voice. I thought I had taken it all in. We parted, me headed for the east wing and her in the opposite direction.

After twenty minutes I was reflecting on how little had changed. The woman was exactly like my old headmistress, albeit transported to another culture. The similarity was enhanced by the fact that both seemed to have been women of image rather than deed. My old headmistress' motto had been that she was always right as long as she wasn't caught making a mistake. This woman had a similar approach. She had given the impression of total self-confidence and inability to be wrong and yet her directions were completely up the spout.

I knew it was her and not me because I got lost within the first five minutes. On the second floor of the east wing I turned right and then left as directed and almost hit a wall – a handsome wall covered with a tasteful mural but a wall nevertheless.

It was downhill from then on. I wasn't helped by the fact that everything in the school seemed to have been named so as to prove to the public that this place was still a cut above the rest – hence the 'east wing', rather than the second staircase; the signs pointing to the 'facilities room' which turned out to be the changing room; the 'retreat' which turned out to be the library; and the office for all enquiries which turned out to be locked.

Eventually I gave up trying to follow my instructions. Instead I relied on my ears. I heard the sounds of animated conversation mixed with the noise of twenty different instruments playing twenty different tunes and I headed towards them.

I arrived in a gym which, with some effort, was doubling as a concert hall. The ropes and equipment had all been packed away but they hadn't been able to do much about the smell of a succession of schoolgirl feet pounding the scuffed wooden floor. At one end of the room was a makeshift stage and on it young musicians were occupying themselves with the kind of finger exercises that wouldn't get in the way of their collective exchange of gossip. Compared to the night before it was a down-at-heel gathering – jeans and T-shirts replaced fancy evening dress, hard energy replaced refined pleasure. It felt much more my style; it had echoes of the jazz venues I habitually frequented. This, I thought, was an evening I might well enjoy. I mention this in passing because it just shows how wrong you can be.

I couldn't see Alicia in the gathering so I asked the first schoolgirl I came across. She shrugged in the direction of one of the exits. I went that way.

Alicia was sitting by a window on a stairwell. She was staring moodily out, her thoughts obviously miles away. When I came up to her and said her name she jumped and clenched her fists. She unclenched them when she saw who I was but it looked as if it was an effort.

'Sorry, Kate,' she said as she reseated herself. 'I was thinking about something.'

'Something interesting?'

'Not really.'

I sat down beside her. I didn't say anything. Alicia didn't seem to mind. She was more at home with silence, this girl, than with speech. I wondered whether that had anything to do with her mother.

I thought about my problem. I needed to get through to her but I didn't know how to begin. I had the feeling that just as Marion Weatherby avoided all physical contact so did Alicia hate emotional closeness. I didn't want to scare her off too quickly but I was getting desperate to find some meaning out of this mess.

'What happened to Richard?' I asked.

'Richard?'

'Your father.'

'Oh, him. I don't know. He disappeared when I was about ten. We never heard from him again.'

'Do you miss him?'

'Oh no. I can barely remember him.'

That baffled me. He left when she was ten and she couldn't remember him? I wouldn't have believed it if Alicia hadn't sounded so sincere. I glanced at her. There was no craftiness in her face; nothing that would suggest that she was deliberately misleading me. True, her voice had a kind of blank, unfeeling character, but it was the type of thing I'd heard from her before.

She must have registered my scrutiny. She got up abruptly. 'I'm always nervous before a concert,' she said, 'and somehow it's worse at school. I suppose it's my two worlds coming together and I think they're going to collide . . .'

She said more than that but I stopped listening. The words she spewed out had one purpose, and one purpose only. They were to keep me away from her. Every time I tried to interrupt, to intervene in what was becoming a hysterical flow, she speeded up. I felt as if I was caught in some kind of mad roundabout which was about to whirl off into space. She must have felt worse.

We were both saved by the entrance of her companion from the night before. He looked angry to see us together and he stood sullenly. Not the best way, I would have thought, to stem Alicia's behaviour, but I was wrong. It worked like magic.

'I was going to come and get you, Pete,' she said.

'Yeah, well I had to run past that caretaker,' he said sullenly. 'You know how he's got it in for me.'

'I'm sorry, Pete,' she said. 'I'm really sorry.'

There was a kind of pleading in her voice – a plea for forgiveness and for help. He ignored it.

'Let's go somewhere,' he said gruffly.

'I'm on soon,' she said.

'Would I ever forget,' he said. 'But you can drink coffee, can't you?'

'Of course,' she said. 'I'm sorry.'

Without a second glance at me they went down the stairs and the sounds of her apology reached me long after they had disappeared from sight.

That was the last I saw of Alicia before the concert began.

It turned out to be a bit of a shambles. For a start the acoustics were just what you'd expect from a gym – worse than useless. In the face of this obstacle the programme consisted of an undistinguished bundle of classical pieces from Stravinsky to Strauss piled helter-skelter on top of each other by an orchestra which couldn't quite make up its mind to play together. It was an exhibition reminiscent of my own sax-playing. Enjoyment, even some skill, was evident, but in the final analysis their technique faltered. Not that the audience minded. Composed of fond parents and sceptical friends, it treated the whole affair as a great night out – not to be taken too seriously but much to be enjoyed.

Alicia was good, though. She alternated between violin and piano and she made music with both instruments. Gone was the violence of the night before, to be replaced instead with a kind of calm confidence which gave depth to her playing without adding the edge that had made me so uncomfortable. She played, in the middle of that hotchpotch of musicians, as if the orchestra was with her – and when she played, the orchestra *was* almost with her.

I sat there and let her music wash over me as I tried to work out why Alicia was so relaxed. Certainly she hadn't shown signs of calm before the concert. Perhaps, I thought, she preferred playing in the midst of this lot, where competition was the last thing on anybody's mind and achievement was finishing the piece on time.

Or perhaps it was the absence of the man. When the concert had started I had searched the audience for him. He hadn't been there. I'd kept half an eye on the door throughout the first half, a duty made easy by the fact that it squeaked every time somebody entered, and he hadn't appeared.

The interval was greeted by rapturous applause followed by a mad dash to the drinks tables which had been set up outside the gym. I stood in front of the choice of wine – red or white – before changing my mind and settling for half of bitter. I took one sip, pushed my way out of the throng and went in search of Alicia.

It was then that I saw him. He was standing by the doors leading to the stairs. He looked as if he were waiting for somebody and he did it with all the confidence that comes from never being let down.

He had the stance of a man who got what he wanted. He was well dressed in a casual way that spoke of wealth. A grey suit outlined a body kept in trim by good living and plenty of exercise. His shoes were polished and Italian – the kind you just can't buy north of Bond Street. He looked like a man without money troubles but not like somebody who worked with money. He was a shade too fashionable for that, a shade too debonair.

I walked up to him, and stood beside him. He didn't acknowledge my presence.

'Just arrived?' I said.

He looked at me and smiled. He had a nice face, open and welcoming – not the kind of face you would expect to terrorise a young girl. He looked too much like somebody's father, somebody's interesting and gentle father who was there to protect and advise. I shook the thought off. It didn't seem like the right time to be projecting my fantasies about fatherhood.

'I saw you last night,' I said. 'Are you interested in music?'

The man looked even more amused. His dark brown eyes twinkled.

'That's one way of putting it,' he said.

'Any music?' I continued. 'Or just the sort made by Alicia Weatherby?'

The man's face changed. Gone was the smile, the casual interest. It was replaced by a virtual shutdown of all expression. He no longer looked like somebody's nice father. He had become, instead, watchful and suspicious.

'Why do you want to know?' he asked coolly.

'I'm a friend of Alicia's,' I answered.

He looked me up and down and he took his time about it. I stood my ground while he did it. It wasn't that difficult. His scrutiny was not at all sexual – on the contrary there was something businesslike about it. I felt as if he was weighing me up and I had to fight a wish in myself that his verdict would be one of approval. The man had a quiet kind of power which made me want him to like me.

I obviously passed the test. He nodded to himself when he'd finished. The coldness left his face.

'Well then, friend,' he said, 'let me reassure you that my

62

intentions are honourable.'

'Maybe you should state them,' I said.

'But how do I know I can trust you?' he said. There was a playfulness in his voice but I guessed the enquiry was a genuine one.

'Sometimes you take a risk,' I said, 'and it pays off.'

The man smiled again and this time I felt there was something familiar about him. I had a nagging feeling that I knew him – that I'd seen him before but in circumstances so different that I couldn't make the connection.

'Risks are part of my business,' he said, 'but I like them minimised. I like to know what I'm dealing with.'

I held out my hand. 'My name's Kate Baeier, and I'm doing some of the worrying for Alicia.'

His hand met mine in a grip which managed to be firm without being too tight. I saw how long his fingers were and noticed the whitened scar that ran by his thumb. That too rang a bell, but too inaudibly for me to make any connections.

'James Morgan,' he said. 'I'm delighted to meet a friend of Alicia's. She needs them.'

There was something in the tone of his voice that made me follow his gaze. He was looking at Pete, Alicia's sullen companion, who was wending his way towards us. There was a roll in his walk and, as we watched, he lost his balance and bumped into a man who was standing to the right of him. The man moved good-naturedly out of the way, making a joke as he did so. Pete turned back to him and muttered something. I couldn't hear it, but I could see the shocked expression on the man's face.

'That one's trouble,' James Morgan muttered.

I wanted to agree but I didn't think it was as simple as that. I still had the memory of Pete comforting Alicia the night before. Trouble he might be, but there was no doubt that he cared about her.

By that time Pete had reached us. He'd managed to clear a path for himself on the way. People he'd passed had instinctively shifted away from his drunken gait. He ignored me and spoke directly to James Morgan.

'She'll see you after,' he said, 'in the sixth-form common room.' His eyes narrowed as he saw me standing there. 'Alone,' he added. And with that he was off.

Morgan nodded to himself, satisfied, at the same time as a hearty-looking type with an old-fashioned beard started ringing a bell. 'Ladies and gentlemen, take your seats. The second half is about to begin.'

James Morgan shook my hand again.

'I have some business to transact,' he said. He gave a wry smile. 'So, unfortunately, I'll have to miss the performance. However, I do hope we can meet again. If you truly are a friend of Alicia's, I'd like to discuss her further.'

He walked briskly away. I thought about following him, about pressing him, but I decided against it.

The second half was a repeat of the first in terms of performance but not in terms of audience participation. The interval had stoked them up and they threw off the yoke of classical silence to show their appreciation of the performers and their boredom at the length of the pieces. It was, all in all, a friendly enough response: it enlivened the atmosphere and wiped out the solemnity that so frequently surrounds 'serious' music. It reminded me of the time I went to see the Bolshoi in Moscow and the audience had shown no scruples about bringing out their sandwiches in the interval.

Whoever had planned the concert had been a pragmatist at heart. They had kept the second half short and dramatic. It was over in forty-five minutes, before the audience could get too rowdy or the participants too rushed.

Alicia came up to me as soon as the clapping abated. She looked more relaxed than I'd ever seen her.

'I'm sorry to give you the runaround, Kate,' she said, 'but there's someone I must see. Can I meet you in half an hour?'

'Are you seeing James Morgan?' I asked.

She looked surprised but unafraid. She nodded.

'Maybe I should keep you company,' I offered.

'Thanks,' Alicia said, 'but this is for me alone. It's all been a big misunderstanding. I'll explain afterwards. See you in the pub on the corner in half an hour.'

She walked away, a spring to her step. I felt pleased for her. For once, it seemed, things were going right in the world of Alicia Weatherby.

The pub was dark and noisy. It was one of those newly-built concrete jobs that boasted a disc jockey and a sound system to match. The man in question was wearing the kind of nylon tracksuit which, if Matthew's school was anything to go by, was all the rage among the under-tens. He was playing music for the same age-group – disco funk that had more beat than sense and where one song merged into the next.

I bought myself a bloody mary and, following the example of the rest of the customers, sat as far from the music as I could.

I lasted the first half hour without much trouble. But after forty-five minutes it got to me – my head began to pound in time to the monotonous beat. By the end of an hour, I could stand it no longer. I got up and left.

The main gates to the school were still open and I walked through unchallenged. It was only as I opened a set of glass doors that led to the main staircase that I heard a shout behind me.

'Oi, you!' the porter called. 'Where do you think you're going?'

I quickened my pace. I had no desire to brush up against him again. He tried to follow me but his breath wasn't in it and as I climbed the stairs, two at a time, his threats became more distant.

'I'm warning you, I'll call the police,' was the last one I heard.

This time I made much better progress. My first journey through the maze of corridors had given me a good understanding of the layout of the place, and I remembered passing the sixth-form common room on the third floor just after I'd reversed myself out of a dead end that was the toilets. I made straight for it.

My footsteps echoed as I moved through the building. The place felt devoid of all life. The dark made it seem even emptier, but I stopped myself from switching on too many lights because I thought that might attract the porter.

I found the room okay, but that was about all. When I opened the door I had to switch on the light before I could see anything.

The room was empty. Only a lingering smell of cigarette smoke indicated that anybody had ever been there.

It was then that I heard it. It was an eerie sound, a kind of keening into the air that was almost inhuman. It was as if a small animal was trapped in terrible pain. It was as if the world had ended. I followed the sound, followed it because it seemed like the right thing to do, even though something inside me wanted to run away from it. It led me across a landing and down two flights of stairs.

The sound was coming from the bottom of the stairs. It changed while I made my journey. From a pent-up agony it had become a series of wracking sobs.

I saw her there as I reached the last landing. She was bending over something, her hand touching something that was lying on the floor.

'Alicia?' I called.

She started and looked up. The sound had not been deceptive. She *was* like a wild animal – her eyes shining in the darkness of the hallway. When I repeated her name she shifted to one side but she didn't move far. It was as if she were hypnotised by the thing on the floor. I couldn't make out what it was. I found a light switch and I clicked it on.

And saw what Alicia had been mourning over. There was a body lying on the floor. The body of James Morgan.

66

Six

He was lying in the most unnatural of positions, one leg bent under the other and his head at an odd angle, but I had to be sure. Gingerly I walked the remaining steps until I stood by the body. I bent down. Alicia sort of scratched at me but there was no strength in her gesture and I easily held her off with one hand. With the other I felt James Morgan's neck. There was no pulse. Already his skin was cooling.

'He's dead,' I said.

Alicia knew already. She stood still. 'I killed him,' she confessed.

She looked me straight in the face, waiting for my response. When I didn't say anything she opened her mouth again.

'I killed him,' she said in a louder voice.

It was then that I came to my senses. Ever since reaching the bottom of the stairs, I'd thought I heard footsteps. I'd suspended the thought while I looked at the corpse, but the footsteps had still been there in the distance. Now there was no denying the sound. And there was a voice to accompany it.

'What's going on?' the caretaker shouted. 'I heard you and I'm coming to see. *Then* there'll be trouble.'

His warning had a kind of frightened quality as if he was using it to chase away any intruders, but his footsteps did not hesitate.

I acted by instinct. I grabbed hold of Alicia and hustled her away from the .body. She came without resistance. I considered leading her back up the stairs but I didn't reckon we'd have enough time. Instead, I pushed her through some swing doors which led away from the footsteps. I forced her to crouch down so she couldn't be seen through the glass pane on the door and then I knelt next to her.

We had moved just in time. The caretaker rounded the corner even as I went down. He must have caught a glimpse of our retreating backs.

'What you doing 'ere?' he shouted. 'It's against the rules.'

His voice stopped abruptly. There was a sound as if he was, with effort, bending down. Then silence for a few seconds.

'Oh my gawd,' he said. He got up. Then the next thing I heard was the sound of him running.

I looked wildly about me. Alicia was where I'd put her, crouched on the ground. I yanked her up.

'Where's the nearest exit?' I asked.

She didn't speak. I shook her roughly.

'We've got to get out of here,' I said. 'He'll call the police.'

Alicia blinked. 'I can't run away,' she said. 'I am responsible. I must be punished.'

I gave up on trying to talk to her. Instead I moved forward, pushing her in front of me. I knew if we went back we would run straight into the caretaker with his police escort.

Adrenalin had made my mind work overtime. They say when you're drowning your whole life flashes before you; well, my experience was a different kind of flash. Suddenly, with a certainty that I would never have questioned, I saw the layout of the whole building in my mind's eye. I knew it as sure as if I'd designed it myself. I pushed Alicia, right and then left and right again through a labyrinth of corridors. I'm sure if I'd stopped to think I would have lost faith, but stopping was the last thing on my mind.

We finally found it, a fire exit that I must have noticed in another world. It was one of those with an iron bar across it so that people could get out and not in. I pushed at the bar. Nothing happened. I pushed again. And again hit steel. It was then that the doubts began to creep in. What was I doing, running away from a corpse with the person who admitted killing him? What was the point, when I couldn't even get her out of the building? I toyed with the idea of going back, of telling all I'd seen, and of walking away from Alicia. And then I looked at her.

I had propped her up against a wall while I tried the door, but she hadn't stayed there. All colour had gone from her face and all resistance seemed to have left her body. She had slid down, until she was sitting, staring up at me. There was desperation in her gaze.

Her desperation fuelled mine. This time I went at the door with a determination and a force I didn't know I had. It worked: the door flung outwards taking me with it. I ran back, pulled Alicia on to her feet and dragged her outside.

Having served its purpose my clear vision of the layout deserted me. I was outside, that much I knew, but that was about all.

'Which way's the back?' I hissed at Alicia.

Alicia pointed in one direction. She even began to move in it. I started running and she followed. Side by side, we left the premises.

I bundled Alicia into my car and drove off. As we passed the front entrance of the school I saw an ambulance pull in, its amber light flashing.

We made it to my flat without further mishap or conversation. On the way Alicia started to shiver uncontrollably. I wrapped my coat round her. She didn't acknowledge the gesture.

She didn't do much of anything until I opened the front door. Sam was there, having come out to greet me when he'd heard my key turn in the lock. Alicia gasped when she saw him. Tears, silent, agonised tears, started rolling down her cheeks. Sam raised his eyebrows and I nodded my head in the direction of the bedroom. He went into it and closed the door.

I led Alicia into the sitting room and put her on the sofa. I removed both coats, mine and hers, but she started to shiver again. I went out, got a couple of blankets, and wrapped them round her.

'I'm going to make some tea,' I said.

She made no sign that she'd heard me. I left her hunched up under the blankets.

When I came back she was rolled into a tight ball. Her eyes were closed. I went up to her and looked: her breathing had slowed and was rhythmical. If she wasn't asleep she was doing a pretty fancy imitation of it. I put the tray down and sat opposite her, waiting.

Sam tiptoed back into the room.

'What's up?' he whispered.

'Tell you later,' I said. 'You better keep out of the way. There's no saying when she'll wake and she had a pretty strong reaction to your presence.'

He nodded and left. 'I'll be in the bedroom if you need me,' he said.

I had plenty of time to think while she slept. I used it in the only way I could – reliving the evening's events. The memory of that broken body kept coming back to me in every detail. I have never been good at painting but that image was so sharp I could have drawn him without hesitation.

I couldn't rid my mind of the image, so I tried to use it. I let my mind dwell on it, and roam free above it. The strategy paid off. Within a very short time I thought I knew why his face had been familiar.

Alicia slept for twenty minutes. When she opened her eyes her first expression was of complete relaxation. She smiled to herself. Then she saw me looking at her and memory returned. She sat bolt upright.

'Have some tea,' I said. 'I'll just freshen it.'

She had first one cup and then another. As she drank, colour began to seep back into her face.

She was looking much better and I reckoned it was time to talk.

'He was James Morgan,' I said, 'the music impresario.'
She nodded.
'What did he want with you?' I asked.
'He was interested in me. He thought I had talent.'
'And?'
'He offered to supervise my progress, to find me another teacher, to, what he called, nurse me to maturity.'

That made sense. James Morgan was famous for finding young musicians and advancing their careers. It had become an obsession with him and, by the sound of it, a very successful obsession. A number of rising stars in the classical music field laid credit for their progress at his door and lately newspapers peddling culture had begun to write about him. He was compared to a Medici – a patron of the arts who spent his energy promoting others. I'd recognised him only because I'd recently seen his photo alongside his life story in one of the Sundays.

He was perfect magazine material. A childhood prodigy, he was on course to become a world-class pianist when he'd developed trouble with his hands. Some arthritis-related disease had crept up on him, paralysing his joints. It hadn't been diagnosed in time. When they'd finally taken measures it had been too late to do anything but sew some muscles together: that was what had caused the scar by his thumb.

He had recovered sufficiently to play the piano but he was never again exceptional. For a while he had disappeared from the music circuit. And then, in the sentimental words of the Sunday journalist, he had decided to give his talent back to the world. He set himself the task of finding young musicians who showed promise but who were not developing as they should. He took them under his wing, and guided them forward. As far as they were concerned, nothing was too much trouble for him. He was said to invest his very soul in his protégés. It was as if he had chosen to compensate for his own loss by making sure that some other young hopeful did not suffer a similar one.

Alicia was a perfect target for him. She could play, that

71

much was obvious, but even in the short time I'd been observing her, my untrained ear knew that the differing moods which affected her music could be her downfall. Virtuoso musicians are allowed to be temperamental but nobody wants one who plays with precision one day and disturbance the next.

If I, basically ignorant when it came to classical music, could have realised this, then James Morgan must surely have understood the problem. It looked as though he had decided to help solve it. And got himself killed instead. It didn't make any sense.

'What happened?' I asked.

'I told you,' Alicia said dully, 'I killed him.'

'How?'

'I pushed him,' she said. 'We met on the stairs and we started to argue and I got angry and I pushed him.'

'How long did the argument take?'

'We started almost immediately,' she said.

'And carried on for an hour,' I finished for her. 'Out on the stairs. When you could have talked in the common room.'

'We meant to,' she said. 'It was locked.'

'Was it?'

Alicia faltered but she wasn't easily deterred. She put down her cup and her face was set hard with determination.

'It's my fault,' she said. 'I killed him.'

'Let's say I believe you,' I said. 'Why did you?'

'I told you. We were having an argument. I pushed . . .'

'. . . all thirteen stone of him down the stairs in a fit of pique.'

'That's right,' she said sullenly.

'You'll have to do better than that if you want to convince me. What were you arguing about?'

'Music,' she said.

'Good enough reason to kill, I suppose.'

That got to her. I should have known it would. I was dealing with a girl whose rules of life were in many ways alien to mine. One of the only constants in her world was music, and she didn't like the fact that I was teasing her about it. Her voice got louder and angrier.

'He said I should be a pianist,' she shouted. 'He said I was throwing away my talents on the violin. That I, of all people, had no reason to give up an instrument because it was more difficult to make a living.'

'That must have really annoyed you,' I said.

She picked up the ring of scepticism in my voice.

'And he was rude to me,' she said in a voice that came closer to a twelve-year-old's than any twelve-year-old's I knew. 'He said some terrible things about my mother.'

'What sort of things?'

'Terrible things,' she repeated.

'So you killed him.'

She didn't answer. She hung her head and she wept softly. I sighed and got up.

'Come on,' I said. 'I'd better take you home. Your mother will be getting worried.'

'What are you going to do?' she asked.

'Sleep on it,' I said. 'I suggest you do the same.'

The fantasy that Marion Weatherby would be waiting up for her daughter was just that – a fantasy. I think I'd had it because I somehow hoped that I wasn't in too deep – that there was somebody else who felt responsible for this mixed-up kid. I should have known better.

We had to ring the bell because Alicia couldn't find her keys. I wondered whether she'd left them by the corpse and what I was going to do about that.

It was some time before anybody answered. When the door finally opened, the maid was standing there. She was wearing a pink fluffy dressing-gown affair and was rubbing the sleep from her eyes. She looked surprised when she saw me, but not over-surprised when she saw who was standing beside me. I gathered that this wasn't the first time that Alicia had arrived home distraught in the dead of the night.

73

The maid opened the door to let us in. Then she began to walk away. I called her back.

'Do me a favour, please,' I said. 'Get Mrs Weatherby.'

The maid looked startled, aghast even. She tossed a silent question in Alicia's direction. I intercepted it.

'It's important,' I said. 'I'll take responsibility.'

The maid still wasn't convinced. She stood rooted in her tracks. I moved towards her and overtook her.

'I'll wake her,' I said. 'Which is her room?'

Neither of them replied. This was becoming tedious. I kept moving.

'Well, I'll try every room then,' I said.

I flung open the first door in the glass panelling.

The maid came running up behind me.

'Don't do that,' she said. 'You will set off the burglar alarms. I will call her. Please wait in here.' She had an accent – an unusual accent that could almost have been Eastern European – and I realised it was the first time I'd heard her speak.

It didn't seem like the right time to discuss her origins so I went into the sitting room as instructed. Alicia followed me. I sat down. She sat next to me, so close that I could feel her breath on my neck.

Marion Weatherby was a quick dresser, I'll give her that. She was with us in five minutes and she was immaculately turned out. Only the lack of make-up on her face showed that she'd been hurried out of bed. That and the fact that it appeared to be an effort to keep her eyes completely open. I wondered what kind of sleeping pill she used.

She cut abruptly into my speculations.

'What on earth is going on?' she demanded. She looked at Alicia. 'I told you we were to have no more of these late night dramatics.'

Alicia moved even closer to me. She whimpered. Marion Weatherby's face softened for an instant. She took a few steps towards us as if she was about to hug Alicia but before she got close enough she stopped. She'd noticed me for what

74

I guessed was the first time. I wondered once again what it was the doctor wrote on his prescription pad.

She scowled at me. 'I hired you to protect my daughter, not keep her out late into the night.'

'I've been doing my best,' I said. 'I think you'd better hear us out.'

She listened as I told her my story – my conversation with Morgan, my projected rendezvous with Alicia and how I had discovered her standing by the body. I left out the bit about Alicia's confessions; they didn't seem appropriate. I needn't have bothered.

'Did you kill him?' she asked.

I knew I was tired and knew I'd been through a lot, but when she asked that question I was astounded. What kind of mother assumes her daughter kills men without provocation? What kind of daughter did she think she had? I interrupted before Alicia could speak.

'Why do you ask?' I said.

Mrs Weatherby was staring intently at Alicia and she didn't take her eyes off her. When she spoke I felt as if her voice was coming from the back of her head.

'Please don't interfere,' she snapped. She reached out and took one of Alicia's hands in both of hers and began rubbing it.

'Did you kill him?' she repeated.

Alicia nodded. Tears flowed down her cheeks.

'You didn't,' I protested.

'I am responsible,' Alicia said.

Faced with a daughter who admitted to the murder of a famous music promoter, Mrs Weatherby did not appear to be the slightest bit put out. She got up briskly. She moved to the door, opened it and shouted one word into the corridor.

The maid appeared. She'd had time to get dressed.

'Run a hot bath for Alicia,' Mrs Weatherby instructed, 'and while she's waiting pour her a small brandy. I'll join you both as soon as I can.'

The maid approached Alicia and stood in front of her.

When Alicia remained sitting the maid bent down and gently pulled her up. The two of them, the one in black and white leading, the other one dumbly following, left the room. Mrs Weatherby called out after them. 'Don't worry, darling. It will be all right. I'll come and give you something to help you sleep.'

Alicia made no sign that she had heard.

Mrs Weatherby had also got up. She smiled at me. 'Thank you for your prompt action in bringing Alicia home, Miss Baeier.'

She stood there waiting for me to leave. I didn't budge.

'Why did you ask Alicia if she killed Morgan?' I asked.

The woman sighed, a long-drawn-out exasperated sigh.

'That should not concern you,' she said. 'My daughter is under my protection and I assure you I will look after her to the best of my abilities.'

'Like accusing her of murder,' I said.

'I did not put the words in her mouth.'

'And I don't think she did it.'

Marion Weatherby smiled, an ingratiating, patronising smile. 'I'm touched by your loyalty.'

'What motive would Alicia have for killing him?' I asked.

'I think she had cause.'

'I have a right to know why,' I said.

Marion Weatherby turned on me. The smiles were gone. She glared at me. 'You have no rights,' she hissed. 'I hired you to protect my daughter, only to find that while under your care, she has committed a brutal murder. One could even say that this makes you an accomplice.'

As she spoke her face hardened. It took on a ghastly, vindictive expression. I felt as though I was at last seeing her true character. I didn't like it; I didn't like it at all. It scared me.

I knew that I should hide my reaction. I stared at her, summoning from my fatigue the energy to pretend that I wasn't frightened by the threat implicit in her words.

She softened immediately. 'Miss Baeier,' she said, 'I do

76

not feel that I owe you an explanation. However, I will attempt to explain. Alicia is a charming child but that's all she is – a child and one with the capacity for destruction. I am not sure that she'll ever grow up. She's flawed, you see.'

'Flawed?'

'She has never been . . . normal.' Mrs Weatherby raised her hand to stop me from interrupting. 'Please, hear me out. Even as a young girl, Alicia was unusual. Perhaps her character suffered because of her extraordinary musical abilities. I have heard it said that geniuses pay a price for their talent.'

'And what was Alicia's price?'

'A certain coldness. One could even call it unscrupulousness. Alicia is not like you and I: she has never abided by common conventions. She can be completely amoral. As her mother I know that only too well.'

I couldn't believe that I was standing there swallowing this garbage. I had only met Alicia a few days before but I felt I knew her well enough to doubt the validity of what her mother was saying.

And yet I did stand there. I'm not sure why. It might have been something to do with the lateness of the hour; it was certainly something to do with the sincerity in Marion Weatherby's voice. Whether I believed her or not there was no doubt that she had convinced herself.

'Are you going to call the police?' was all I said.

'I will consult my solicitor,' Mrs Weatherby said, 'and act as I think fit. And now, I would like to see to my daughter.'

This time I got up. There didn't seem any point in staying to engage in double-talk with the woman.

I walked to the door. As I reached it, Mrs Weatherby's voice followed me. 'You had better wait until I phone downstairs,' she said. 'Otherwise the porters might well take you for an intruder.'

It was almost three o'clock when I reached home. Sam was making a brave attempt at propping his eyelids open. 'What's

77

going on?' he muttered in his half sleep.

I told him, the uncensored version this time, along with my undiluted opinions of Mrs Weatherby's behaviour. By the time I'd finished he was fully awake.

'Why do you think she didn't do it?' he asked.

'Why should she?' I asked. 'He was offering her help and if there's one thing Alicia Weatherby needs, it's help.'

'But maybe she couldn't bear what he offered because it was too much and she's too deprived of love. So she killed him, and with him her need,' Sam suggested.

'Oh, please,' I said, 'spare me the amateur psychology. I've been through enough tonight.'

'But that's what they say, isn't it?' Sam continued. 'People kill for either love or money. And it sounds like Alicia Weatherby has enough money.'

I got into bed and pushed him playfully. 'Give us a break. Psychodynamically the motive might make sense but who acts out like that? Especially an eight-stone girl against a substantial man. She didn't do it.'

'Well who did, madam detective?' Sam asked.

'Search me,' I said. 'Maybe he fell.'

'Did he fall or was he pushed?'

'Corny,' I said.

'It's three o'clock in the morning. What do you want? Poetry?'

'It might help.'

'Come closer, then,' he said, 'I'll whisper some in your ear.'

I got closer. As I began to lose myself in physical sensation a part of me stood back and watched. That part judged me. Was it true what they said: that there was an intimate connection between sex and death? I saw a corpse, heard a confession and then jumped into bed with my boyfriend.

I chased the judgments away. I'd had enough of the fight between morality and immorality for one night.

Sam spoke once before closing his eyes for the night.

'Careful you don't get burned,' he said. 'You're not one of them, don't forget that.'

78

Seven

Carmen said much the same thing, but more forcibly. When I arrived in the office at half ten she took one look at my face and got to work on the coffee percolator. She listened in silence to my story.

She wasn't so silent after I'd finished. Her face had grown stormier and stormier throughout my narration and she was bursting by the end.

'Those people are the limit. They're parasites who're using you for their own ends. Keep away from them. They'll squash you like an ant if it serves their purposes.'

'Yeah,' I agreed, 'but I feel responsible. For Alicia. She's different.'

Carmen pursed her lips together, and then opened them to expel a dismissive breath.

'Who you kidding?' she said. 'Sure, Alicia's different. She's young. She's in training. Give her a few years and she'll fit right in there.'

I had expected a negative reaction from Carmen but the bitterness in her voice seemed out of proportion. I looked at her curiously.

'Why such a passionate denunciation?'

'I don't trust those people,' Carmen said. 'I never have.'

'I know that,' I said. 'But something's made you angrier.'

'Marion Weatherby phoned before you came in,' Carmen explained. 'She left a message. She doesn't even want to talk to you. Effectively what she said was thank you and goodbye. Send her your bill, a reasonable one, you understand, for services rendered, and she'll pay. She doesn't want you contacting her daughter any more.'

'Oh,' I said. I was taking in two things at once – the fact that Marion wanted to part ways and the fact that this was no reason for Carmen to get so angry.

Carmen looked at me fiercely. '"Oh." What's that supposed to mean?' she asked.

'All I said was "oh".'

'Don't play the innocent with me,' Carmen said. 'It's not like you to take this lying down.'

I didn't say anything.

Carmen had one more shot. 'Don't expect me to bail you out of this one. It's strictly private. Between you and the rich.'

I didn't understand what was going on. Granted, my mind was fogged by lack of sleep but still, I thought, Carmen was truly over-reacting. I wondered whether her anger was to do with yesterday and whether she had transferred her disappointment from me to Marion and Alicia.

'About yesterday . . .' I tried.

'Forget yesterday!' Carmen shouted. 'I have work to do.'

She glared at me. I resisted the temptation to drop the matter.

'Any news about Elmore?' I said. I tried to keep my voice casual.

She wasn't fooled. 'I warn you, Kate. Give it a break.'

'But this is business,' I argued. 'Jarvis is business. Our business.'

Carmen snorted. 'I'm working on it,' was all she said.

The rest of the day passed slowly. The silence in the office had a quality I didn't like but didn't know how to change. Carmen worked on her cases and I on mine. When we needed to communicate we did so with maximum politeness and minimum warmth. It made me unhappy and I guessed from the number of sighs emanating from her desk that Carmen wasn't exactly overjoyed either. I concentrated on my paperwork while fighting my drooping eyelids.

At four o'clock I looked up to see Carmen standing over me. She was smiling.

'You've been asleep for half an hour,' she said. 'Not even the telephones woke you so I've put the answerphone on. I'm off to see Elmore. I'll ring in and leave a progress report. Why don't you go home and get some rest?'

I nodded and returned the smile.

'I'll just clear up here,' I said.

Carmen left and I spent a quarter of an hour alternating between washing coffee cups and splashing cold water on my face. It was an effort to wake up properly. Eventually I got myself organised enough to leave the office. I closed the door behind me.

It was while I was still locking up that I felt a hand grasp my shoulder. It held me in a grip that I knew only too well. I turned to face the owner.

It wasn't really that I knew him – more that I knew his type. He was short-haired and badly kitted out. He was wearing a badly fitting brown suit and a pair of highly polished brown shoes that were made for kicking. There was an expression of malice on his over-large face. He looked like a nasty piece of work. He had a companion with him. At that moment, I couldn't tell them apart.

The one with the arm action was spokesperson.

'Kate Baeier,' he said in a loud voice.

'Who wants to know?'

For an answer he took something out of his breast pocket and flashed it quickly in front of me. All I saw was a glint of silver.

'Come with us, please,' he said. The last word seemed to have been tacked on to make things even more sinister.

'Do you have authorisation?' I asked.

The man went for an imitation of a smile. His lips parted; his teeth were bared.

'Don't give us any trouble. We don't like trouble. Do we, Jim?'

Jim grunted and moved round to my other side. He, too, put a hand on my shoulder.

'Are you arresting me?' I asked.

'Do you want us to?' the first man said.

'You can't do this,' I protested.

Jim decided that it was time to speak. His contribution hardly thrilled me. 'Can't we?' he said. 'I'd have thought that somebody of your background would know all about the PTA. I bet you even demonstrated against it. Now you have the pleasure of seeing it in action.'

They'd used up their supply of words and they resorted to action. I was hustled down the stairs and into a waiting car. There was a uniformed policeman in the driver's seat which was some relief to me. At least, I rationalised, these men were genuinely from the police force, but what did the Prevention of Terrorism Act have to do with me?

The plain-clothes men sat on either side of me in the back seat. I had been protesting all the way down the stairs and into the car and they'd maintained a stolid silence. Now, out of earshot of the public, they weren't so shy.

'Vocal, isn't she?' Jim said.

'Can't say I like 'em that way,' the first man answered. 'What do you think?'

'Oh I don't know, Terry. I like a bit of spirit.' Jim leaned towards me and flicked his hand under my chin. I tried not to react but instinctively I flinched from his touch. The two men chuckled.

They went on like that all through the journey. Baiting me, touching me, crowding me. I knew that this was the beginning of the tactics of intimidation but knowing did not make it any the easier to bear. I was beginning to feel dirty, polluted by their presence. At one point I caught the uniformed man's eyes in the front mirror. I thought he looked disgusted but maybe I just wanted to imagine having an ally in that crowded car. He certainly didn't say anything.

He drove to the back of the Essex Road police station and stopped the car. He stayed seated while Jim and Terry hauled me out. He avoided my gaze while they pushed me into the building.

I was taken through a bewildering maze of corridors, all of which stank of urine and bad food, and through an unmarked door. I was pushed on to a hard chair and told to be a good girl and sit. The room was bare and windowless. The only other furniture in it was a scratched table with a second chair behind it.

Jim and Terry stood behind me and carried on with their double act. I'd got used to it now, and it didn't seem so threatening. Or maybe it was because they weren't so physically close to me that I was able to relax.

I felt a blast of cold air as the door behind me opened. Jim and Terry went silent and I tried to turn to see who had entered. I was prevented by a rough hand on my head.

There was a whispered conference behind me and then someone crossed the room and sat behind the table. He was a man in his early fifties who carried authority with confidence. He was one up on the social ladder from my other two companions, his suit was tailored rather than off-the-peg, but that didn't make him reassuring. His face was grey from over-consumption of cigarettes, and hardened by over-exposure to the police force. It was a square, bitter face, with eyes which were too small to blend comfortably with the whole.

He had a file with him. He opened it and looked through it. Then he closed it, leaned backwards so that his chair was tilted, supported by the wall, and stared at me.

He stared at me for what seemed like a long, long time. I stared back. 'I demand to know why I'm here,' I said. 'I want to make a phone call. I want my lawyer.'

'Got a loud one here, haven't we, boys?' the man said.

'Been going like that all the time, sir,' Terry answered. 'Someone needs to shut her mouth.'

'I want to make a phone call,' I said.

'All in good time, girlie,' the man said.

'You can't hold me like this,' I said.

'Can't we just?' he answered. 'You're behind the times. You've not been swotting up on our new powers have you? Thought this country was soft, compared to where you come from, didn't you.'

He'd said it casually but he watched closely for my response. He was testing me, testing to see whether his knowledge of my history would threaten me. It did. But then I told myself to relax. Let's face it, a naturalised British citizen from Portugal was probably one of the easiest of people to trace in the police computer.

If he was disappointed by my lack of response, he didn't show it. Instead, abruptly, he changed tack.

'Let's have your movements during the last week,' he ordered. 'I want to know where you ate, slept and washed. I want everything. And be quick about it.'

'I want to see my lawyer.'

'We call them solicitors here,' he sneered.

'I have a right to a phone call.'

'Only if you've been formally arrested. You're only what we call helping the police with their enquiries. Don't you know anything? How long did you say you'd been in this country?' He looked through the file again. I could see that he wasn't really concentrating on what was written there.

I was quietly going crazy. I didn't understand. Why had they pulled me in? Had something happened, something that I didn't know about? Had my past in Portugal finally caught up with me?

He saw the confusion in my eyes and he smiled. 'We have witnesses, you know,' he said. 'And plenty of them.'

'I demand to make a phone call.'

The man sighed. He closed the file. He spoke over my head.

'Just my luck,' he said. 'She's going to be difficult. Get her out of my sight. She makes me sick.'

I was dragged from behind and hustled out of the room. I was pushed down yet more corridors and into a place where the doors clanged when they were shut. I was forced to wait while a uniformed cop used two keys to open one of them. Then I was shoved inside.

'I want to make a phone call,' I said, before they could shut the door.

Terry smiled. 'Keep quiet,' he said. 'Or I'll give you a phone. Right up your cunt.'

The door banged shut. I heard them laughing as they walked away.

I was in the cell for an hour. Not a second more or less. It felt like somebody was programming my visit, somebody with an obsessive attention to detail. Thinking about it later I'm pretty sure the hour was just a coincidence but it shows the kind of thing you can start being paranoid about when you're left alone in a police cell.

The man who let me out was uniformed and carrying a huge bunch of keys.

'Where are you taking me?' I asked.

He shrugged his massive shoulders in the direction of the door and pushed me towards it.

'I demand to use the telephone,' I said.

He didn't bother to reply.

I was pushed into a room which was empty of furniture but seemingly full of people. There were six of them there – all women. They were standing in a rough line-up. When I entered their eyes swivelled towards me and then, as quickly, turned away.

'You can stand where you want,' the policeman said, 'just don't take all day choosing.'

I looked at the line-up. They were women of all shapes and sizes. Not one of them remotely resembled me.

'I object,' I said. 'I demand to know why I'm here. I demand to speak to my solicitor. I want my rights. I want to make a phone call.'

The policeman sighed. He pushed me into the line.

'You better stop talking or you'll be identified by your noise.'

I stood in the line and shut up. There didn't seem anything else to do. I'd spoken up in an attempt to see whether any of the women would be sympathetic towards me. The way they had concentrated their gazes – on the ceiling, the floor, each other, anywhere but on me – had given me my answer.

We stood in line for a very short time and then the policeman was back.

'That'll be all,' he said. 'Thank you, ladies.'

We started to shuffle towards the exit. He caught me before I could leave the room.

'Don't even think it,' he said. 'I've no escapes on my record and you're not going to change that.'

I was shown into another interrogation room. It was different from the first in that the walls were grey rather than dirty pink, but otherwise it was identical. My interrogator from the previous interview was there, already seated, and the duo that had kidnapped me were propping up the wall.

I made a move to sit on the second chair but I was prevented from doing so by Jim who used one hand to grab me by my hair and the other to move the chair away. When he let go there were tears in my eyes. I tried to ignore them.

The senior policeman had been doing his file reading act again. Now he looked up and smiled.

'You might as well come clean, Kate,' he said in a tone of voice that was trying hard to be kind. 'We've got all the evidence we need.'

'I want to see my lawyer,' I said.

'You've been identified by the caretaker,' the policeman continued. 'He'll testify that you were there twice that evening. He saw you enter the second time but he never saw you leave.'

'I want to make a phone call,' I said. My mind was working overtime. The caretaker – so that was it. They had pulled me in because of James Morgan. I should have guessed earlier but I hadn't because I hadn't wanted to work out what I was supposed to do. I cursed myself for my lack of forethought. Of course the caretaker would remember me.

But hold on a minute. So the caretaker had identified me: who told him my name? How had they known where to pick me up? What, I thought, had Marion Weatherby done now? Had she implicated me in order to conceal her daughter's complicity?

'We don't want to be hard on you,' the policeman said. 'There are other things we will find. We'll get at least twenty witnesses who saw you talking to Morgan earlier in the evening. We know you were with him and we know you pushed him. Tell us why. We're on your side. Were you lovers?'

'My lawyer,' I said.

'We won't go for first degree if it wasn't premeditated,' he said. 'But we can only help you if you help us. Yes?'

The last word he barked out. I thought at first that it was directed at me – as some sort of bizarre order that I should contribute one of my two sentences – but when I turned round I saw that a policewoman had entered the room. She went up to the man by the table and handed him a note.

He read it and frowned. Then he read it again, and again he frowned. He looked up.

'Get her out of here,' he said. 'Fast.'

I was manhandled out of the room and into the corridor. There I was left to stand, guarded by the ever-present Terry. We didn't have to wait for long. Jim came out of the room, tossed his head at Terry in some kind of buddy-code and the two of them pushed me towards the back entrance.

I was flung into a black maria whose windows were darkened. The doors were slammed shut. I banged but nothing happened. I waited in the dark and then I heard the sound of the engine being switched on. The van lurched off, and me with it.

We drove for about fifteen minutes before the van came to an abrupt stop. The doors were flung open. I blinked into the light, trying to make out where I was. We had stopped in another car park, similar to the last. I had been shunted to another police station.

I was shown to a cell, locked in it, and left to my own devices. I paced it. I sang in it. I read its walls. I hopped around it. I shouted at it. I stared at the stew that had been shoved at me and I gave back the full plate when requested. I demanded my statutory phone call every now and then, and I lay on the bed and stared at the ceiling. It was very, very boring. Thank God that, in one of the staring sessions, I managed to fall asleep.

It was an uneasy sleep, interrupted as it was by strange echoing noises. But I must have closed my eyes for a good six hours. I could only make a guess as to the time for my watch had stopped dead, as if protesting at the turn of events.

I can't say that when I finally admitted defeat and stopped pretending that I could sleep, I felt rested. The boredom had gone, replaced by a sense of defeat. I couldn't understand why Sam hadn't come and got me out. The awful thought that he didn't even know where I was crossed my mind and, to drive it out, I banged on the cell door again. No one responded.

It was a good two hours before I saw anybody. I'd long ago given up banging when a fresh-faced young man in a blue shirt that had been starched so as almost to stand off him, opened the door and grimaced at me in my slept-in clothes.

'This way,' he said.

'I demand a solicitor,' I said, as I followed him.

'Don't you all?' he cracked.

'You're cynical, aren't you?' I said. 'Are you practising for when you grow up?'

He turned round to face me. He'd gone red.

'Watch it,' he said, with more swagger than conviction.

He took me into one of those ubiquitous interrogation rooms and let me sit down while he guarded me. We were silent there for about half an hour before the senior plain-clothes man from the previous police station came briskly in.

'You've been lucky, Kate,' he said. 'We've had a confession.'

He held up his hand to stem the tide of words that were about to issue from my mouth.

'Now, I know what you're going to say,' he shouted. 'But before you do, let me warn you. You start throwing accusations about police brutality and incorrect procedure and we'll want to know exactly what you were doing in that school and who you were with. We might even charge you with wasting police time and concealing evidence. We'll tie you up in court and it won't only be you that gets hurt.'

He stood up so that he was towering above me.

'And don't think I won't do it,' he said. 'We have a note circulating now that will follow you round. It says that if Kate Baeier is brought before the authorities for any reason, any reason whatsoever, then I, Inspector Crant, will hear of it.'

He nodded to my guard. 'Get her out of here,' he said, one final time.

Sam and Carmen were waiting for me when I was released. They both looked terrible, as if neither of them had had any sleep, but the glances they threw my way told me that I looked worse. I hugged them both.

'Thought you weren't going to bail me out,' I said to Carmen.

She laughed and squeezed my arm.

'Let's go and eat,' I said. 'I'm starving.'

We came out into weak sunlight on to a street I'd never seen before.

'Where the hell are we?' I asked.

'Tottenham,' Sam said. 'They moved you when our solicitor found out where you were. It's taken half the night to catch up with you again.'

'Who confessed?' I asked.

'Let's go eat,' Carmen said. 'And maybe you should have a bath.'

We went to my flat and I sank into as much water as my tub would hold while I drank two cups of coffee and salivated at the smell that Carmen and Sam were jointly creating in the kitchen. We didn't make too much conversation while we tucked into a meal of omelette, fried potatoes, tomatoes, rye toast, coffee and plenty of orange juice. The two of them seemed as hungry as I was. Either that or they were just exercising their jaws on the food so that they wouldn't have to talk.

I pushed my plate away. 'Who confessed?' I asked.

They looked at each other.

'I'll find out some time,' I said.

Again their eyes locked. I waited out their silence.

'Peter,' Sam said eventually.

'Alicia's boyfriend?'

They nodded.

'What did he do?' I said incredulously. 'Walk into his local police station and come clean? Couldn't stand the thought of my incarceration for a crime I hadn't committed?'

'Not exactly,' Sam said.

I was in full verbal flood. It must have been something to do with the release of tension and the limited conversations I'd been having in the previous twenty hours. Whatever the reason, I ignored their warning glances and carried on.

'Don't tell me,' I said. 'He was really a publicity-seeker at heart. He saw how famous James Morgan was and he phoned the press.'

Carmen interrupted. 'He OD-ed,' she said.

That stopped the flow.

'Dead?' I asked.

'He killed himself,' Sam said.

'How would anybody know that?'

'Because he left a note confessing to Morgan's murder. He said it was a mistake. He did it in a jealous fit when he thought Morgan was going to take Alicia away from him for good.'

'Long note,' I commented.

They didn't say anything. The silence hung there, oppressive.

90

I needed time to digest the news. I changed the subject. 'How did you know I'd been arrested?' I asked.

'I tried to get hold of you,' Carmen said. 'First I left a message in the office and then at home. When I didn't hear from you I had a feeling something wasn't right so I contacted Sam.'

'We did a bit of detective work,' Sam said proudly, 'asked around at your office. Mr Singh from the travel agent said he saw you leave with two men who looked so much like thugs that he guessed they were policemen.'

'Then we got Colin, you know, the one from the law centre, to find out where you were. When we arrived at the police station we discovered that you'd been moved and no one would own up to knowing where you where,' Carmen said.

'They went to a lot of trouble for a common or garden murder suspect. They could have just held me as a material witness, instead of all this moving about. I thought it was odd at the time.'

'Maybe they were doing somebody a favour,' Carmen said.

The whys were beginning to pile up and I didn't have the answer to any of them. If Marion Weatherby had given my name to the police then how could she expect to do it without incriminating Alicia? And shifting me from one place to another seemed dumb – what was that supposed to achieve? It didn't make any sense.

And there was something else that didn't make sense.

'I don't believe it – about Pete,' I said. 'Junkies don't leave notes and conveniently go and overdose. Or confess to crimes. Their whole life is denial.'

'So what?' Carmen snapped. 'Leave it alone now.'

'How can I?'

'Because it's over.'

'You think I'm going to give up? None of it makes sense. I want to know why I was imprisoned. I want to know what's going on.'

'Why? Because you were held in a police station? It happens to my people all the time. They've grown used to swallowing it and getting on with their own lives. What makes your experience so special?'

I was finding it hard to believe my ears. I had never heard Carmen talk in such a defeatist way. I looked at her and she looked back at me. There was no friendliness in her face – only the type of regard one would expect from a stranger. I couldn't understand what was happening – we were staring at each other from across a huge divide. If we couldn't solve this one quick, something would be gone from our relationship for ever.

I took a deep breath. 'Look here, Carmen,' I said. 'I'm sorry about the other day. I was wrong. I should have asked you straight out to see Elmore. It was my own feelings of guilt that prevented me. I acknowledge that. But, for god's sake, aren't any of us allowed to change? Okay, so it's hard on you. But just don't start with this crap about our people and your people and swallowing things. I don't believe in that and I don't believe you do either.'

My speech had the most miraculous effect on Carmen. Instead of walking out as I feared she would, or throwing me a look of stony incomprehension, she smiled – a lovely, warm, open smile. 'So there's life in you after all,' she said. 'I was beginning to wonder.'

I was on the verge of getting angry again. I wanted to shout at her, to tell her that I wouldn't be patronised. But then I saw in her face that there was gentleness and a kind of approval. I had disappointed her the other day: she was telling me now that it was all right. I returned her smile.

'Now that's solved,' Sam chipped in, 'let's drink alcohol.'

'It's only ten in the morning,' I protested.

'Yeah, after what a night,' he said. 'And I suspect that, with the two of you going into action, the day's not going to be much better. What would you like?'

Eight

The alcohol turned out to be not such a bad idea. It acted on my neck muscles, mellowing them so that the stiffness began to fade. It helped, for a moment, to push the thought of death and destruction away from the centre of the stage. But the trouble with alcohol is that its effects are always temporary. After about an hour I was worrying again.

I picked up the newspapers which lay unopened beside me. I flicked through them, pretending to myself that this was an idle scanning, at the same time as I searched out the obituary columns.

James Morgan's death was reported in both the *Guardian* and *The Times* and in much the same way. They described how he had been found in the school by the caretaker and how the police were investigating but suspected that he had fallen by accident. His illness, it was implied, might have made him dizzy. Otherwise both papers sang the praises of a patron of music cut off in his prime. The list of virtuosos that Morgan had encouraged made impressive reading. His death, said *The Times*, was a tragedy for music; the *Guardian* called it a calamity.

That was about all I gleaned. The funeral was pending a post mortem, but would be sure to be held within a week. A concert, commemorating Morgan and performed by his protégés, was also in the offing.

I looked up at Carmen when I'd finished with the papers.

'What was the message?' I asked.

'What message?'

'The one you left in the office. About Elmore.'

93

Carmen groaned. Sam echoed her. He picked up a piece of paper that was lying beside him, crumpled it into a small ball and threw it my way. I ducked.

'So what was it?' I asked.

'I went to see him,' Carmen said. 'I had a lot of difficulty getting in but eventually I persuaded him. He's a physical wreck and nervous with it.'

'I noticed,' I said.

'He was in a fire,' Carmen said, 'the fire at Jarvis's factory.'

I sat bolt upright.

'That's it,' I said excitedly. 'A compensation scandal.'

Carmen cut through my enthusiasm. 'Afraid not,' she said. 'According to Elmore, Jarvis's firm has been more than generous to him. They paid for private medical care – can you imagine it, that black boy in a private hospital – they sent him to a convalescent home and they're supplementing his income until he's able to work again. After that, they'll give him his job back.'

'It doesn't make sense.'

Carmen groaned again. 'You just looking for trouble on this one, girl. Let it alone.'

'But it doesn't make sense,' I insisted.

Sam agreed. 'Whoever heard of a firm like that being so spontaneously generous?'

Carmen sighed.

'I suppose so,' she said. 'Looks like I'm due back on Elmore's doorstep.'

'And I on the Weatherbys',' I said. 'But could you do me one more favour?'

'Could I refuse?'

'Find out who Crant is. An Inspector Crant. I got a feeling that he's involved in something unsavoury. What he did to me went beyond the cause of duty.'

Carmen nodded.

This time when I walked into the entrance hall the doorman

must have been expecting me. He pointed to the sofa and asked me to sit. He used his phone and when he'd finished he just stared at me. I stared back.

Neither of us blinked when the lift arrived. Out of it stepped a man in his mid-fifties. He, too, looked vaguely familiar, though I had no idea where I could have met him before. He had an urbane air about him that must have come from years of practice. His face was small and pointed, his sandy brown hair retreating from the forehead, but he let none of that get in the way of an overall impression of certitude. He strode towards me as if he'd measured his pace already and knew exactly how many steps he needed to get within shaking distance. He stuck out a hand.

'Miss Baeier,' he said, 'Allow me to introduce myself. Name's Plastid, Trevor Plastid. I am the . . .'

'Weatherbys' lawyer,' I said.

He smiled. 'Extremely observant of you. But then, you are a detective . . .'

There was a slight query at the end of his sentence that I chose to ignore.

'Let's talk,' I said.

'Naturally.'

'Upstairs.'

'Ah,' he answered in a voice poignant with regret. 'Unfortunately, that is impossible. It goes without saying that Mrs Weatherby is grateful for your efforts on her daughter's behalf but she feels that there is nothing more that can be done. I do apologise for your fruitless journey. I was assured that a message had been transmitted through your secretary. I'm certain you will understand.'

'Sure,' I said. 'I understand.'

He put his arm round me in a gesture which was nicely tuned to the fraternal, and he started to steer me towards the exit.

'The trouble is,' I said, 'I'm not going along with it.'

He stopped and looked at me, puzzled.

'The thing is,' I said, 'I'm in a bit of a quandary. I've had very little sleep in the last two days and that always make my quandaries worse. I am liable to act rashly when I really get a quandary going.'

He interrupted. 'Your personal life is of no concern to me. I have tried to be kind but, I warn you, should you persist in interfering in the life of my client – or that of her daughter – you will leave me no option but to act.'

'What would you do?' I asked. 'Arrest me and have me locked up? I thought that's where I came in.'

'What are you implying?'

'I'm sure you could work it out, given time,' I said. 'Let me get back to the quandary. As I said, I'm tired. In all the time I could have been sleeping I wasn't and, given that police cells are notoriously uninteresting, I had to use the time for something. I chose thinking.'

'Get to the point,' the man said.

'This is the point,' I said. 'I have been held in jail and I have been released from jail. I have been very clearly warned by the police that, should I choose to protest my incarceration, they will drag Alicia's name through the mud. The police are clever: they know I might not want that for reasons of loyalty – loyalty to my employer. You, however, are not being so quick on the draw.'

'That's blackmail,' Plastid stuttered. I was pleased to see his face flush.

'Call it what you like,' I answered. 'I'm not proud.'

He was a good loser, I'll give him that. He wiped the rancour off his face and rearranged his features. He even squeezed out a smile. 'Be so good as to wait here,' he said. 'I will inform Mrs Weatherby that a further consultation is desirable.'

He walked off briskly and took the lift up to the fifth floor. I saw it return almost immediately. Trevor Plastid was standing in it. He beckoned to me.

'My client will see you now,' he said. 'I ask you to make allowances for any confusion you might encounter. As you must understand the household is in some disarray.'

If the Weatherbys were in disarray they certainly didn't show it. When I entered the huge sitting room mother and daughter were both there, flicking through magazines. Marion smiled and inclined her head in the direction of a lone seat they seemed to have imported for the occasion. Maybe they thought that a jailbird would leave a mark on their nice sofas.

Alicia also greeted me. She looked at me as if I were a stranger popping in to distribute leaflets. I thought she might be in shock but when I looked closer at her eyes I saw that they were clear and untroubled. That irritated me.

I'd barely had time to sit before Mrs Weatherby got down to business.

'I'm confident,' she said, 'that Mr Plastid has passed on our gratitude to you, Miss Baeier, for all you have done.'

'He did mention something,' I said.

'Then I'm at a loss to understand the purpose of this meeting,' she said plaintively.

My irritation increased. The Weatherbys – mother and daughter – were really beginning to get on my nerves. I was no longer interested in the wide repertoire of their mood-swings. I'd been through too much to tolerate it.

Trevor Plastid must have noticed me grimace. He cleared his throat and shot a warning glance in Marion's direction. These two patently knew each other well. He was telling her to cool it.

His warning took effect. Marion tried another tack – the gracious hostess number this time.

'Your incarceration must have been thoroughly un-pleasant,' she said. 'An acknowledgment of that fact will be reflected in your fee.'

'I don't think I've yet mentioned money,' I said.

'Well, I cannot understand what else you want,' she said.

Trevor leapt in before I could retort.

'I do believe Miss Baeier is correct, Marion,' he said. 'Money does not seem to be at the front of her mind. If I understand her correctly, she merely welcomes this opportunity to clear the air. As do we all.'

'What air?' Marion Weatherby asked. She sounded genuinely confused.

I raised my voice. 'This air,' I said. 'The air in this room. The air that led you to assume your daughter killed a complete stranger and that led you to the conclusion that the way to get her out of trouble was to implicate me. The air that made sure I couldn't be tracked by my friends.'

'I have no idea to what you are referring,' she said.

'Well, try harder,' I was shouting now. 'Because this isn't going to get us anywhere. You had me arrested. I know it was you because who else could have identified me to the police so quickly? Who else knew where they would find me? Two nights ago I told you the whole story, porter and all. Funny how the porter came so promptly to an identification parade. You probably even supplied the police with a copy of my fingerprints taken off one of your bone china cups.'

'I resent that,' Mrs Weatherby said.

'You mean they're not china?'

The solicitor intervened. 'Miss Baeier has a point, Marion,' he said. He looked at me and smiled. He seemed to be trying to get me to sympathise with him for having so difficult a client. But he was doing more than that: he was going all out to placate me.

'I am positive that, in different circumstances, Mrs Weatherby would want to apologise sincerely for all the trouble you have encountered.' He continued, 'I am also certain that you will understand that her actions were motivated by the primary concern of a mother for her daughter. I do not intend to belittle the deprivation you have suffered, but the matter can surely rest now that it has been satisfactorily cleared up.'

'Because you conveniently found another murderer,' I said.

For the first time since the conversation began, Alicia reacted. She let out a small sound of pain. I glanced at her. Her head was bent low, concentrating on her hands, which twisted and turned on each other in her lap.

'Don't do that, darling,' her mother said. 'It is so unattractive.'

I spoke directly to the solicitor.

'I need to ask Alicia some questions,' I said.

'We have no objection to that.'

'In private,' I said.

He looked dejected. 'I'm afraid that's impossible.'

I gave in. I didn't have the energy to fight and I'd heard a hint of steel in his voice which meant that he wasn't going to concede easily. I raised my voice in an attempt to attract Alicia's attention.

'You told me you murdered James Morgan,' I said. 'Was it true?'

Alicia shook her head. She did it for longer than was necessary.

'Did Pete do it?' I asked.

'Pete's dead,' Alicia said.

'I know. Did he kill James Morgan?'

'He must have,' Alicia said. 'He said he did.'

'He told you he did?'

'No.' Alicia's voice was so soft that I had to strain to hear it. 'He left a note.'

Mm, I thought, the note. I steered her away from it. 'What happened that night?' I asked. 'Tell me from the beginning.'

Alicia's brow furrowed as if it was an effort to remember. 'James Morgan asked to see me,' she said. 'And when I realised who he was I saw how silly I had been to be scared of him. So I agreed to meet him.'

'In the sixth-form common room,' I said.

She nodded. 'Pete showed him the way,' she said. 'And then James asked him to leave us alone. Pete didn't like that.'

'The boy was jealous of Alicia, jealous of her talent,' Marion Weatherby said.

Something flashed in Alicia's eyes. 'That's not true,' she snapped. She was silent for a minute. 'It's not true,' she repeated in a voice of defeat. 'Pete was pleased for me. He wanted the best for me.'

'So he left you alone with James Morgan,' I prompted.

Alicia nodded. 'He said he would wait for me at the end of the corridor.'

'And then what happened?'

'James and I talked,' she said. 'I liked him. He was so nice and friendly. He asked me a whole lot of questions and he seemed to understand all my answers. He knew, you see, what it was like to want to play – really play I mean.'

Alicia's face took on a far-away look. She was reliving her conversation with Morgan, revelling in the memory of how somebody had been genuinely interested in her. I thought I understood: James had appealed to me, and Alicia, without a father to help her, must have gone overboard for him.

'Why had he been following you?'

'He hadn't,' Alicia replied. 'Not really. He'd been coming to my concerts to see whether I was good enough. He wanted to help me in my career, you see. He told me I had talent. He even said I should concentrate on the piano.'

'Did you agree?'

'It's what I always wanted,' she mumbled in a voice so tiny that I might even have imagined it.

Trevor Plastid coughed in the background. He was trying to tell me that we were getting sidetracked. I forced myself back to the business in hand. 'How long did you talk to James?'

That didn't please Plastid either. 'Is this entirely necessary?' he asked impatiently.

'It's all right, Trevor,' said Alicia. 'I don't mind. We talked for about half an hour. We worked out what to do. He said he would persuade my mother. And then it was time to meet you.'

'So you both left?'

'No,' Alicia said and her voice cracked in the saying.

I waited. Nothing else came out.

'You left alone?' I prompted.

'No,' she said. 'I didn't.'

There was only one more option available.

'James Morgan left first,' I stated. 'Why did he do that?'

'I wanted to think about what he had said. He suggested that I should. So he told me that he would tell Pete to wait a bit and then come and get me. I'm scared of the dark, you see.'

'And?'

'I waited and I waited. At first I didn't notice time passing because I was so happy. And then I got worried. I was scared I'd be locked in the school. So I went to look for Pete.'

'Did you find him?'

'I found James,' she stuttered.

'Was he alone?' I asked.

She nodded. And then, at long last, she began to sob. As the tears flooded down her face she did nothing to staunch their flow. She was crying for all she was worth, crying out her pain, her loss and her anguish. It was hard to witness without wanting to walk away from it. Out of the corner of my eye I saw Marion Weatherby move as if she was going to interfere but Trevor Plastid stopped her with a shake of his head.

It was a long time before the sobs subsided. During that time the three of us stayed quiet, witnesses to Alicia's desolation. Marion stared out of the window, Plastid rustled papers as if he were reading them and I focused on a spot on the Persian carpet in front of me. I looked up only when I was sure that Alicia had cried herself to a standstill.

I was shocked by what I saw. Alicia was in the process of drying her eyes with her sleeve. She smiled at me: she actually smiled! Was I imagining things or did I see a look of triumph in that smile? Had all that crying, I wondered, been nothing but another well-tuned performance? I was assailed by doubt. Perhaps her mother was right – Alicia was essentially amoral. I had never thought her the most well balanced of people but this was incomprehensible.

I told myself that I was being stupid – that grief was

unpredictable. I concentrated on finishing the questions.

'When did you last see Pete?' I asked.

'Haven't you done enough?' Marion shouted. 'Leave her alone.'

'I might as well finish,' I said.

There was a silence from the adults that I took to be consent. I looked at Alicia.

Alicia's voice was poised in comparison to her mother's. 'Last night,' she said.

'Did he tell you he killed James Morgan?'

Alicia shook her head.

'Did you tell him *you* killed James Morgan?' I tried.

Another shake, less definite this time.

'Why did you tell me that you killed him, then?'

'I don't know,' Alicia whispered.

I wasn't convinced. The scene I'd just witnessed had thrown me into confusion. I no longer trusted Alicia and I no longer trusted my own impulses in regard to her.

I knew I needed time to think. I changed tack. 'Did Pete seem depressed?'

'Pete was often depressed,' Alicia said. 'He had a difficult life. I'm tired. Can I go now?'

'One more question,' I said. 'Why did you hire me?'

Alicia looked startled but not as startled as her mother, who put her hands on her hips and spoke down her nose. 'There is a limit, Miss Baeier,' she intoned. 'You know why we hired you. We did not know who James Morgan was and we thought his intentions might not have been honourable.'

'I'm surprised Alicia didn't recognise Morgan,' I said. 'Even I remembered his picture from the papers and I'm not a musician.'

'My daughter is too busy to read the papers,' Marion Weatherby said.

'Be that as it may,' I said. 'My question was why Alicia chose me to investigate.'

'I really cannot see the point of this,' the mother said.

'But Alicia can, can't you?'

I had directed the question straight at her and I watched her closely for her response. She bit her lower lip.

'I don't know what you mean,' she said. The voice was not in her usual repertoire. It was nearer the five-year-old mark.

'Neither do I,' her mother said. 'I think you have done enough harm.'

I could have pushed, I know, but I decided against it. The dead were dead and nothing would revive them. I had plenty of time, I thought, to find out. And anyway, I didn't think Alicia would tell me in front of her mother.

So I dropped it. I got up and said my goodbyes. There was nothing but relief on their faces as I left the sitting room.

Trevor Plastid, after a hurried consultation with Marion, followed me down the hall.

He opened the door for me.

'I am so pleased we have cleared the air,' he said. 'And hope you appreciate my client's position. There is no need for further investigation. I'll be sending a letter to this effect but, in the meantime, please accept my words as verbal instruction from Mrs Weatherby.'

He stood to one side to let me out.

'And thank you so much for your assistance,' he said.

When I got downstairs I took a deep breath. I was in shock. All the time I'd been busy despising Marion Weatherby I hadn't really given Alicia much thought. Now the contradictions in her behaviour came flooding back. Two people close to her – one a stranger who had offered a desperately needed helping hand, the other her boyfriend – had died and yet she was prepared to let it be.

I didn't like it. I didn't like it at all. But I had to face the fact that there was nothing I could do about it. I needed more information.

I picked on the nearest person. I walked up to the doorman who was closeted in his cubicle.

'I am sorry, miss,' he said when I got right beside him. 'I didn't notice you there.'

103

I bet, I thought. Confusion was making me malicious. 'Don't apologise.' I tried a gracious smile.

'Do you want something?' he asked.

'Have you worked here long?'

'Who wants to know?'

'My name's Kate Baeier,' I said. 'I'm employed by the Weatherbys.'

'That's not how I heard it,' he said. 'Word is that they've given you the sack. About time too if you ask me. What the police can't deal with is best left alone in this life, that's what I say.' He breathed peppermint all over me and leered.

'Yeah, yeah,' I said and put up my hands in a gesture of resignation.

I walked away. There was no point in continuing. I'd approached him because I suspected that he would know as much about the people who lived in this building as anybody else. It was obvious that I was right. It was also obvious that he would tell me nothing.

There was a coffee shop opposite the building. It had large glass windows with a full view of the main entrance and it was giving off an aroma that made my nostrils twitch. I went inside, ordered a cup of Mocha from a choice of five different varieties, slugged it down and ordered another. The second cup I nursed in my hands as I bit into a freshly baked croissant made from pastry so thin and layered that it flaked pleasantly in my mouth.

I kept a casual eye on the Weatherby building. I watched as Trevor Plastid came out, knotting his black scarf around his neck. He hailed a taxi and got into it, giving his instructions like a man in a hurry. The taxi sped off and I soon lost sight of it.

Nothing else happened for a while. The croissant had sent messages to my stomach so I ordered a toasted cheese and ham sandwich which arrived along with a choice of three mustards. I chose Dijon. It all went down pretty well so I ordered another.

I was on the last mouthful when the maid came out. She

walked briskly along the road, letting her brightly coloured cape swing round her as she went.

I didn't reckon I had anything to lose. I dropped some loose change on the table and ran out of the place before anybody could stop me.

She was walking fast, her legs stretching out in long gracious strides. I ran behind her, scared that if I shouted I would frighten her off. It wasn't easy following her. She walked with purpose and with luck – every time she wanted to cross a road the light was green for her. Not so for me. I had a few narrow escapes and picked up a number of irate comments before I caught up with her. I was still in full motion and I grabbed roughly at her to stop myself.

She turned round with a fierce look on her face. It didn't stay there for long. When she saw who it was, she laughed in a friendly enough manner.

'It's you,' she said. 'He did warn me.'

'Who did?'

'Fred,' she said.

She saw my blank look.

'The porter,' she explained. 'He told me to watch out for you. I gathered you were pumping the help.'

'He didn't like it. Do you feel the same?'

She laughed again. 'I hope I never do,' she said. 'He's a crawler. Thinks he'll get treated better if he does what he's told. More fool him.' She shrugged and her cape opened to reveal a patterned Peruvian jumper. 'How can I help you?' she asked.

I suggested we go find somewhere to talk and she readily agreed. I was still puffing from my exertions so we chose the nearest place. It turned out to be a cross between a tea-shop and a wine bar, divided into two distinct sections. She was, she said, after the wine part, so I followed her into the back.

I chose orange juice. She studied the wine list. She looked completely different out of that black-and-white uniform. Her skin had lost its pallor and her face its diffidence. It was as if she came alive when she walked out of the Weatherby apartment. It wasn't only the bright colours that contrasted with the starkness of her uniform – it was something more, something alive in her face. I felt as if I was confronting a truly free spirit. It was a great relief after Marion's coldness, Alicia's hysteria and Trevor Plastid's polite and stony front.

She knew her wines and she took her time about choosing. She gave her order to the waiter with authority and she waited for him to serve it right. She tasted the first mouthful and gave a sigh of appreciation.

'It's one of the things I miss most,' she said. 'Good wine, good food.'

'You come from Hungary?' I asked.

'Not bad.' She held up her glass in a mock toast. 'How did you know?'

'I've got a Hungarian friend,' I said. 'Your accent's familiar. She came out with her parents after '56. Why did you leave?'

She grimaced. 'The worst reason,' she said. 'For love.'

'So where did he go?'

'I married an Englishman,' she said. 'I thought he was exotic. He seemed exotic in Hungary. But in England I realised that he was just as parochial as every other Englishman.'

'But you're not going back to Hungary?'

'It's been a long time,' she said. 'I was a bit slow at getting rid of him. Only just managed it. He wouldn't leave the flat. I had to go.'

'Is that why you took a live-in job?' I asked.

She nodded. 'Just till I find my feet,' she said. 'Now tell me, what do you want to know from me? I have a language class to attend.'

'Your English seems pretty good to me,' I said.

'I'm learning Chinese,' she said. 'I thought it would be useful to have a sixth language under my belt.'

She watched as I blushed. I could see she was enjoying herself.

'I want to know something about the Weatherbys,' I said.

'Like what?'

'Like where Richard Weatherby is. Is he dead?'

She frowned as if she were thinking hard. 'I'm not sure, I've never seen him.'

'Could he be dead?'

She shook her head. 'I wouldn't think so. I once heard Mrs Weatherby refer to him. She spoke with such venom I assumed he was still alive.' She paused and spoke the next sentence as if she didn't quite understand where it was coming from. 'And I feel his presence.'

'In what way?'

Her face cleared. 'Probably my imagination. Living with those two can get you thinking all kinds of crazy things.'

'What goes on between Alicia and her mother?' I asked.

'There's a question,' she said. 'They fight like cat and dog. It's not normal. Me, I fought with my mother, but with them it's something different. Like some chasm from years back that they never could solve.'

'What do they fight about?'

'You name it. About what instruments Alicia should play, about what Alicia should eat, about boyfriends, about men . . .'

'Men like Gordon Jarvis?'

She smiled. 'Him too when he was on the scene.'

'He's left?'

'Marion gave him the push the other day. It's her normal pattern. She won't let anybody get too close to her. Plenty have tried it – she's got looks, money and charm – but she's ruthless. None of them can stand the pace.'

'What does Alicia think of a constant stream of men?'

'She doesn't like it. Not that she is allowed any say. Marion keeps Alicia out of the way almost as if she's confining her to the nursery. That, I think, is why Alicia has never properly grown up and is such a mess.'

'Mrs Weatherby is not in such great shape herself,' I said.

'What do you expect? She takes too many drugs.'

'Like Pete,' I reflected out loud.

'Maybe that's why Alicia chose him.' The maid looked at her watch. 'Got to go,' she said.

She smiled at me and then left. She left me holding the bill for her very expensive glass of wine. There was a woman who knew what she was doing.

I paid and decided to call it a day. The tiredness that I'd been fighting could no longer be kept at bay. I went out on to the street, hailed a taxi and sank back into it.

It was only four o'clock in the afternoon but I was practically asleep when I got back to my flat. It was empty. Sam had left some flowers – three pink carnations so delicately edged with blue they could have been hand-painted, surrounded by a spray of gypsophilia and a note. 'Gone to try and work,' it read. 'Four phone calls – Carmen and three hang ups.'

The bed beckoned me. I thought about having my second bath of the day to really get me in the mood for sleep but I decided it was too much of a risk – I was so exhausted I might drown in it. Instead I made straight for the horizontal.

'Nothing will stop me sleeping,' I said aloud.

It was then that the phone rang. Automatically I picked it up.

It was Carmen on the other end.

'Kate,' she said. 'I got the story from Elmore. And it makes interesting telling.'

Nine

'Where are you?' I asked.

'Not far,' Carmen said. 'We'll be over soon.'

I thanked her and put the phone down. No sooner had I done so when it rang again. I picked it up and said hello.

'Kate,' said a seductive voice on the other end. 'It's Toby.'

'Toby?'

'Toby Stafford. We had a drink the other day.'

'Oh, hi,' I said. 'Have you been hanging up on my boyfriend?'

'I was hoping he wasn't,' he said. 'Although that's not necessarily an obstacle, is it?'

He said it casually, with just a slight inflection on the last two words. I wasn't in the mood for his game and I didn't have the strength to tell him quietly.

'I'm really not in the mood for this,' I said.

He was a good loser, I'll give him that.

'I've called at a bad time,' he said quickly. 'I do apologise. Perhaps another day?'

'Yeah, perhaps,' I said.

He hung up apologising sincerely. And at that point the doorbell went.

I stubbed my toe while going for the button to let them in. Fatigue and the Weatherbys had made me irritable and I was cursing as Carmen and Elmore made slow progress up the stairs. I was reaching the stage where I didn't care any more – wasn't interested in what Gordon Jarvis had done to Elmore or how many people dropped dead around Alicia Weatherby.

One look at Carmen's face was enough to stem my ill-temper. She was smiling and there was an infectious kind of triumph in her smile.

Some of Carmen's sense of victory even seemed to have rubbed off on Elmore. He came in puffing from the effort of hauling himself up the stairs, but his face wasn't quite as defeated as when I'd last seen it. He smiled at me and I thought I could detect the first glimmer of a healthier man from a healthier time.

'Thanks for coming,' I said.

He smiled again. 'Carmen hammered some sense into me,' he said. 'Plus she gave me some guarantees.'

I tossed an enquiring glance at Carmen.

'I told Elmore that anything he tells the two of us doesn't go any further. We have to keep quiet about the whole thing unless we can find corroborative evidence that leaves him out the picture.'

That seemed fair enough. I nodded. 'Take a seat,' I said. 'I'll get us a drink.'

I came back into the room carrying three cups: coffee for Elmore because he said he was hooked on the stuff, camomile tea for Carmen and peppermint tea for myself because I find camomile too glutinous. Elmore and Carmen had made themselves comfortable while I'd been in the kitchen. They were rooting through my record collection comparing notes and criticising the gaps in it.

I gave them their cups and waited for them to get adjusted to my presence. I had a feeling of being a stranger in my home – of being somehow out of sync with the rapport they'd established – but I told myself that it was only to be expected. As Carmen had been at pains to tell me, I'd sent her to Elmore because I thought the colour of her skin would make him less suspicious: I couldn't now expect that Elmore would automatically transfer his trust to me. Fatigue, I knew, was making me over-sensitive so I sat there, tasting the burn of the peppermint, and feeling sensitive.

It didn't go on for long. Carmen looked up, saw the drift of my face and put down the Billie Holiday album she'd been holding. She turned to Elmore.

'Tell Kate your story,' she said. 'Just as you told me.'

His face, which had livened up while he was showing his expertise about jazz singers, closed again.

'You stand by Carmen's promise?' he asked.

'I do.'

He used the arms of the chair to pull himself up. He limped over to the window and stared out of it. His voice sounded as if it was coming from a long, long way away.

'I worked at Mately's for six months,' he said. 'Soldering one piece of transistor to another. The work was hard on the eyes, and the pay wasn't much, but it was a job and after two years on the social you aren't that fussy.'

He paused and took a deep breath.

'One day while I was at work I smelled fire. It happened so quickly, it was all around me by the time I even realised I was in danger. I lost consciousness. Only reason I got out was that one of my mates came back for me. He carried me to the window and threw me out before jumping himself. I was lucky.'

He waved one of his crutches in the air as if he wanted to beat the window, or maybe himself, with it. His voice dropped so low it was almost a whisper.

'My mate wasn't so lucky,' he said. 'I never got to thank him. He died in the inferno.'

'What happened?' I asked.

'I told you,' Elmore shouted. 'He died.'

'Was there an investigation?' I asked.

'Sure there was,' he said. 'I was in hospital for weeks but my mum went to Tommy's inquest. Said everything was done above board and Mately's offered compensation to Tommy's wife. He had two kids, you know. Mately's was very generous – Jarvis himself saw to that. Just like he saw to me, offering me sick pay and a job when I get better. What choice did we have? She took the money: so did I.'

I looked at Carmen and saw my sadness echoed in her

face. But her expression wasn't a complete replica of mine. I felt confused, as if I were missing something.

She saw my confusion and she dug into her bag. She pulled out a piece of paper which she unfolded. It turned out to be a large photocopy and she spread it on the floor in front of her. I knelt beside her.

It was a set of plans, drawn to scale. I looked at it hard. It meant nothing to me. I looked at Carmen.

'I got this from the council,' she said. 'It's the latest plan of Mately's. Drawn up before the fire and approved by the fire authorities.'

I looked again but her explanations hadn't clarified anything.

'So?' I said.

'Elmore and his friend had to jump from a second-floor window,' she said.

'So?' I was growing impatient. I wished Carmen would just come out with it.

'Look again,' she said.

This time I examined the plans more closely. This time comprehension dawned. 'No second floor,' I stated.

'Exactly,' Carmen said.

'So what happened?'

'Mately's was doing well,' Carmen explained. 'All the YTS people meant that Jarvis could cut his labour costs down to a minimum. Only trouble was, he didn't have room for them all.'

'He solved that soon enough,' Elmore said. 'He had a second tier built in the factory. Knocked a hole in the ceiling so there was just enough natural light, along with the fluorescent strip, to make the job possible. The heavy machinery was kept downstairs – the light jobs on the second layer which was made of wood. We got to it by climbing up a steel ladder. Mately's henchmen said it was a temporary measure until his relocation grant came through.'

'Which turned the place into a fire trap without any safety exits,' Carmen finished.

112

'And nobody complained?' I asked.

Elmore grimaced. 'We knew it was dangerous but what could we do? I did ask the environmental health man who came round once about something. He said I should report it to the fire department. He also said that if Mately's didn't comply with the fire regulations and do some expensive repairs, they could slap a closure order on him.'

'And that wouldn't make it cost-effective,' Carmen chipped in. 'So they'd all lose their jobs.'

'Instead of our lives.' Elmore limped back and sat heavily in his chair. He put his head in his hands and sat there quietly.

I wanted to do something. I wanted to go up to him and make it better. I wanted to tell him it wasn't his fault. I wanted to get Jarvis. Carmen saw what I was thinking and she warned me off with a shake of her head. So I too sat there, my mouth shut.

It was Carmen who broke the silence. She got up and went over to Elmore. She touched him lightly on the shoulder.

'Thanks for coming,' she said. 'I'll get a taxi to take you home.'

He looked up.

'I'll take a bus,' he said.

I nearly protested but another look from Carmen prevented me.

'Are you sure?' she said.

He lifted himself up. 'I got to start living again,' he said. He nodded to me and then, haltingly, he left the room.

'Is he going to be okay?' I asked Carmen when she came back from helping him down the stairs.

'As okay as life will allow,' she said.

'You gave me a lot of keep-off warnings,' I said.

'It was an effort to get Elmore to talk about it. He feels guilty about his friend's death and about surviving. It's easy for that guilt to turn to rage and I was scared that an expression of outrage from you would tip him over.'

'I suppose you're right,' I said. 'But what are we going to do?'

'Nothing without corroboration,' she said. 'Remember your promise.'

'So what's next?'

'One of us should go talk to Tommy's wife. If we could get her to open the case again, we'll be getting somewhere. And what about your resident depressive?'

I frowned. 'Who?' I asked.

'The computer man.'

'Who?' I said again and then the penny dropped. 'Oh, you mean Jonathan Blenter.'

'That's right,' she said. 'Ask him if he's heard anything about Mately's.'

'Why him?'

'My, we *are* alert,' Carmen said. 'Because the Hardwick PC might have used Mately parts. So Jonathan Blenter could have heard something of interest.'

'I'll try him,' I said. 'I just hope he hasn't done himself in. That's all I need.'

'Speaking of death, what happened at the Weatherbys'?'

'They gave me the push. The way they reckon it, with James Morgan no longer bugging Alicia and Alicia no longer in danger of being caught as his murderer, I'm superfluous to requirements.'

'Does Alicia agree?'

'Who knows?' I said. 'I've lost all idea of who Alicia is and what it is she wants. First she finds a dead body and then her boyfriend kills himself and she carries on acting little girl lost. Maybe you were right – I should give up on them.'

Carmen was incredulous. 'What? Even with the Jarvis connection?'

I sat back in my seat and sighed. I stretched my legs out in front of me and felt the muscles uncramping.

'I'm beginning to think that the Jarvis connection is just a red herring. A strategy by a thwarted youngster to get a little revenge.'

114

'What do you mean?' Carmen asked.

'Well, suppose Alicia somehow gets to overhear Gordon Jarvis telling Marion Weatherby that Baeier Investigations is annoying him with time-wasting enquiries. Picture the conversation – after-dinner drinks – safe topics including the iniquities of London boroughs. So Gordon laughs about us. Now Alicia has picked up that all's not kosher in Mately affairs. So she chose me as her detective, in the hope that not only will I solve her troubles, I'll also throw Jarvis in the shit.'

'That's a lot for her to overhear,' Carmen said.

'I get the impression that she's not got much else to do around the house except practise and eavesdrop. And there's so much trouble between her and her mother I can just imagine that she took delight in interfering in Marion and Gordon's relationship. The maid says it's over between them now. Maybe Alicia succeeded in pushing Jarvis out of the picture. Didn't want her mother to have a lover.'

'So,' Carmen reflected, 'you think it all boils down to sex?'

'Make a change, wouldn't it?'

Carmen got up. 'Well,' she said. 'I must be going.'

'Speaking of sex you must be going – or just you must be going?'

Carmen smiled again. 'Wouldn't you like to know?' she joked.

'I think I just got my answer,' I said. 'Go smile somewhere else, hey? Us old married people need our sleep.'

Somehow I found the energy to ring Jonathan Blenter and ask him if he could investigate. He agreed to dig out what he could about Mately's without much enthusiasm.

'I suppose it'll stop me dwelling on my own problems,' he said doubtfully. 'Why do you want to know?'

'Oh this and that reason,' I said. 'Tell you another time.'

He didn't press it. I knew he wouldn't. In the final analysis Jonathan was interested in one thing and one thing only – himself. Everything else was a bit of an effort and gratefully skipped, given the excuse.

I put the phone down and went to sleep. Just like that. At six o'clock in the evening. No dilly-dallying – fast asleep where I sat.

I was woken by a sharp breath on my shoulder and a sweet smell under my nose.

'Look what we bought you,' Matthew said.

'More flowers,' I said. 'Lovely.'

'Matthew insisted,' Sam said. 'He wants all the gory details of your visit to the police station and the flowers are a bribe.'

'Some sleep might work better,' I groaned.

Matthew wasn't having any of it. He didn't literally pour iced water over me but he made damned sure that closing my eyes was one of the last options in the world. Nine-year-old persistence is, in my experience, pretty persistent and I soon gave in. It was a hard story to tell since Matthew's emotional inclination was to go with my version while his intellectual upbringing, courtesy of the TV, was to identify with the police. But somehow he made his own compromise with the conflicting ideologies – enough at least to get me to retell the whole tale while he drank in the details.

'I would have eaten the food,' he announced. 'You could have been there for a long time.'

'Yeah, but you probably would have liked the food,' I said. 'I haven't forgotten that you eat school dinners.'

'They're delicious,' Matthew shouted and then turned on the TV before I could dispute it.

I closed my eyes.

The flat was empty when I next woke up. The table was laid for one and there was a note beside the plate.

'Food in the oven,' it read. 'Took Matthew home. See you tomorrow.'

I went to the oven and switched if off. I didn't have the energy to open it, or the energy to eat what was inside. I went back to sleep – this time in my own bed.

116

Ten

I dreamt I solved the murder. It was very satisfying. Sam and Carmen watched in admiration while I told them how James Morgan had been asphyxiated by a violin string and that Pete was not dead but merely hiding from a false accusation made by Inspector Crant. I picked up the telephone to ring Marion and congratulate her for getting rid of Gordon Jarvis.

But instead of hearing the dialling tone, the phone began to ring. I shook it but that did no good. I woke up and picked up the receiver.

'I'm terribly sorry to disturb you at this time,' a polite voice on the other end said. 'But it is . . .'

'What time is it?'

'I beg your pardon? Oh . . . I see. I'm afraid it's nearly four.'

I groaned.

'Miss Baeier,' the voice said, 'are you there?'

I groaned again. 'This had better be good.' The words were coming easier now and I clasped the phone more firmly to my ear. I eased myself into a sitting position.

'It's Trevor Plastid,' the voice said. 'Marion Weatherby's solicitor.'

'What happened?' I asked. 'They kill somebody else?'

His voice became sterner. 'I will ignore that,' he said, 'given the lateness of the hour.'

'Big of you,' I said. 'So what's up?'

'Marion Weatherby is very concerned. She has been burgled.'

117

This time I didn't bother to conceal my groan. 'Tell the police. I believe they run an all-night service.'

I hung up. I turned over and shifted my weight about the bed, preparing to return to my dream. The phone rang again.

'If this isn't very, very important,' I barked into it, 'I won't be able to answer for my actions.'

'The problem is,' Plastid said, 'that Mrs Weatherby does not feel it wise to inform the police. Some extremely valuable items have disappeared.'

'Call the insurance company,' I said, 'although I'd wait until the morning if I were you.'

'And Alicia has gone too,' he said.

I sat up abruptly. 'When?'

'This afternoon,' he said. 'After we both left. Marion says that Alicia became rather distraught. Words were exchanged and she rushed out. At first Marion wasn't concerned. Alicia has been through a difficult time recently and Marion thought she needed to be alone. She expected Alicia to return when she had calmed down. But when Marion discovered the burglary, she went into Alicia's room. Alicia wasn't there.'

I was out of bed with the receiver resting on my shoulder as I pulled on some jeans. I stopped myself. Hold on, I said to myself, where do you think you're going? I sat back on the bed.

'Why don't you try Alicia's friends?' I asked. 'I certainly have no idea where she is.'

There was a hesitation at the other end of the line. When Plastid spoke again his voice was apologetic.

'We cannot,' he said. 'We have no idea where to start. We would be immensely grateful if you could discuss it with us.'

'On one condition,' I said.

'Name it,' he said quickly. Too quickly.

'I'm not a disposable item,' I said. 'This time if I'm hired I stay hired. The job's over when I say it's over.'

The lawyer in Plastid couldn't take that. 'Surely,' he said, 'there is a conflict of interest here. The right to terminate a contract is at the very basis of our society.'

'It's ten past four in the morning,' I said. 'I am not interested in society's rights. Take it or leave it but, whatever you decide, let me off this phone.'

'Agreed,' he said.

'I'm on my way.'

The doorman was waiting for me when I arrived. He held the door open for me and threw me a dazzler of a smile. I guessed he was hoping I'd forget our previous conversation now that I was once again in vogue.

'You work all hours,' I said, thinking that if he was prepared to mend fences, who was I to get in his way?

'I'm on a late shift,' he gushed. 'As a favour to the night man. I shouldn't be doing this, I should be in bed.'

'I know how you feel,' I said.

He talked right through my comment. There was something he wanted to say and he was not going to let anything get in the way of the telling of it.

'I was here all the time and I didn't see anybody. I swear I didn't see anybody. You tell them.'

I looked at him more closely. He was in quite a state: he was sweating slightly and his face was suffused with anxiety. I thought I recognised the mark of Marion Weatherby at work.

'After your blood, are they?' I asked.

'I was here all the time,' he repeated.

I nodded and started to walk towards the lift. He didn't like that. He put out a hand and stopped me.

'Tell them,' he said. There was an angry edge to his voice. I wasn't in the mood to deal with it.

'Okay,' I said. 'Let me go and tell them.'

He didn't like that. He held on tighter and put his face close to mine.

'Don't toy with me,' he said.

I'd had enough. I took a deep breath like they'd always instructed me in the self-defence class and I moved my arm fast. It worked like a dream. He wasn't expecting resistance and he let go. Taking advantage of his surprise, I strode over to his cubicle. I reached into it and under the shelf. I brought out a half-full bottle of gin. I held it up to him.

'Is this what scares you?' I asked.

The doorman made no attempt to reclaim the bottle. Instead he swallowed convulsively as if something was stuck in his gullet.

'Don't worry,' I said. 'It's not my job to lose you yours. Just don't try pushing me around.'

'How did you know?' he asked.

'Peppermints,' I said. 'Every time I came.'

I replaced the bottle and then stepped into the lift.

Trevor Plastid was waiting for me on the fifth floor. 'We're extremely grateful,' he said.

'Good,' I said. 'Got the contract?'

He frowned. 'Surely my word is enough?'

I turned to go.

'All right, all right,' he said petulantly. 'Come inside and I'll draft something.'

He ushered me in and then, as if to show that his usual politeness had deserted him under the strain of my demands, he left me standing in the hall. He walked through an opening in the mirror wall into what looked like a study. When he came out he was holding a piece of paper. He handed it to me.

'I trust this will suffice,' he said.

I looked at it. On the paper was scrawled a piece of legalese, the drift of which was that I now had a contract with Mrs Weatherby to investigate matters to be discussed verbally, the contract to be terminated by mutual agreement between the two parties. It also bound me to some pretty stringent vows of secrecy and confidentiality for good measure. I grinned to myself – this, I thought, was Trevor Plastid's way of being a good loser.

'This seems fine,' was all I said. I folded the paper and

stuck it in my pocket.

Plastid ushered me into the living room. Marion Weatherby was already there, seated in one corner of the vast space. She was a changed woman. She was slumped into the sofa and she made no attempt to sit up when I entered. She was dressed neatly enough but she looked completely different. All the gloss, the glamour and the care were absent. It was a lesson to me – a lesson in how much work it takes to preserve a Marion Weatherby image and a lesson in how quickly it can be lost. I'm sure the lesson was not new to Marion.

She smiled at me when she saw me sit down. It was a smile of recognition and it looked as if it had been quite an effort to produce it.

'Thank you,' she said. 'You must find our behaviour difficult to understand.'

I shrugged.

She reached for a teapot that had been placed to her right. Her hand trembled as she did so. She used the other one to help her steady it.

'Would you care for something?' she asked.

I shook my head.

She poured herself a cup. Halfway through the action she gave up concentrating and some liquid spilled out on to the table. She didn't even notice. She put the cup to her lips and gulped at its contents. She grimaced.

'Foolish me,' she said. 'It's cold.' She shivered as if to illustrate the sentence. 'I've had quite a shock,' she said conversationally.

Trevor Plastid had sat down next to her. He looked embarrassed. When Marion failed to say anything more he couldn't contain himself. He coughed, once softly and the second time loudly. The cough got stuck somewhere and when he spoke his voice was hoarse.

'Marion,' he said. 'Perhaps we should tell Miss Baeier what happened.'

'You're always so practical, Trevor,' she commented.

'I do my best,' he replied. He'd done his best to keep that sentence neutral but he couldn't hide the slight edge in his tone. I didn't blame him. Marion looked as if she had been going on like this for quite a while and five o'clock in the morning was probably stretching the limits of even the most faithful of family solicitors.

'Ms Baeier must think that we are a peculiar family,' Marion said. She lifted the cup to her lips again. She sipped and then looked at Plastid speculatively. 'I suppose we are,' she said. 'What do you think, Trevor?'

'You've had your troubles.'

'What happened?' I asked.

Marion threw me a sly smile. It wasn't only sly: it was also devious and childish in its deviousness.

'Wouldn't you like to know?' she said. 'Wouldn't we all?'

'I mean, what happened last night?' I said. 'And where do you think Alicia has gone?'

'Ah, Alicia.' Marion Weatherby pulled a face. 'My daughter. My darling, darling daughter.' She leaned forward. 'I know what you're thinking,' she said. 'You're thinking that I'm not a very good mother. Well perhaps you're right. I won't argue with you. But it's not all me.' She shook her head and pointed a finger at herself. 'Oh no, it's not all little me. Alicia played her part. And Alicia plays to perfection. Have you heard her?'

While she was talking Trevor Plastid was showing signs of increasing discomfort. He shifted in his chair, he cleared his throat, he twined his fingers round each other, he looked around. Now he could stand it no longer. He got up.

'I'm calling your doctor, Marion,' he threatened.

Marion Weatherby looked coldly at Plastid. Her childishness evaporated and was replaced by control tinged with contempt.

'Sit down, Trevor,' she said. 'Don't make a fool of yourself.'

She turned back to me. 'I went out last night,' she said. 'I got back at midnight and went to bed.'

'Was Alicia here?'

'I have no idea,' she said. 'I was tired out and I went to bed. I managed to get to sleep but at three I was awakened.'

'By a noise?'

'I don't know,' she said. 'I have, for some years, had trouble sleeping and I do occasionally wake in the early morning. It does me no good to lie worrying, so I got up and came into this room to pour myself a drink. Even then I might not have noticed if it hadn't been for the draught. I hate draughts. I have never been able to abide the cold.'

She'd had a kind of confiding tone in her voice when she said the last sentence and I was scared she was going to drop back into whimsy.

'So this particular draught disturbed you,' I prompted.

She nodded. 'I went to find its source. I followed it to the front door. The door was open, wide open. Have you noticed,' she asked Trevor, 'that the temperature in the hallways is less than adequate?'

This time she saw the look on my face before I could say anything. She got on to the right track all by herself.

'I hadn't noticed anything out of place and so, although I was annoyed, I wasn't unduly worried. After all, we pay our doorman to keep an eye on the building. And it's not the first time that this has happened. I assumed that, once again, Alicia had been careless.'

'It could have been the maid,' I said.

She shook her head. 'Oh no, Eva would never do that. I went into Alicia's room to speak to her about it. She wasn't there. I thought she might have gone out again. It was only when I was pouring myself a night-cap that I saw it was missing.'

'What was?' I asked.

She looked vaguely at me. 'The vase,' she said as if I already knew.

'A Ming dynasty vase that usually stood on the mantel-piece. An item of considerable value,' Trevor Plastid contributed.

'Anything else?'

She hesitated before she spoke. 'No,' she said finally.

'Why don't you call the police?' I asked.

'I couldn't possibly do that,' she said. 'Don't you understand?'

'Not exactly,' I said.

She sighed as if I was being wilfully stupid.

'This was no ordinary robbery. Alicia took the vase.'

'Why would she do that?'

'For revenge,' Mrs Weatherby said. 'To get at me. She knew I didn't like her to handle it.'

'You're very quick to accuse your daughter. We've already been through murder. Now we're on to theft.'

'Who else could have done it?' she asked impatiently. 'The doorman swears that only residents entered the building.'

I didn't say anything but she must have detected my look of scepticism.

Her voice rose. I wondered who she was trying to convince. 'The appartment was not broken into. Alicia used her keys,' she said.

'Which she'd lost,' I said. 'The night James Morgan was murdered.'

Marion Weatherby looked startled, genuinely startled. An expression of fear crossed her face – an expression which reminded me of Alicia.

'Alicia is always mislaying her keys,' Marion protested, 'only to find them in her bag. And there are also spares in the kitchen.'

'Why don't we check,' I suggested.

She looked at me, confused.

'To see if the spares are gone.'

She got up. 'Of course,' she said. 'Follow me.'

I was led into the corridor of mirrors and down it. It was quite a walk, made long by the dazzle of reflections as we passed.

The kitchen was huge, furnished with all mod cons, but soulless. Stainless steel surfaces gleamed, empty of food, implements or love. An enormous fridge hummed in one corner, outdoing the freezer it faced. The place was spotless and the counters virtually unscratched. It bore all the signs of money spent without thought. Somebody who didn't care about kitchens, who didn't like to cook, had gone out on a spending spree and kitted it out so they would no longer have to think about it.

The maid was sitting hunched over the table.

'Why don't you go to bed, Eva?' Marion Weatherby instructed.

Eva gathered up her books and began to leave. Before she did so, she threw a look in my direction. I nodded and cast my eyes down.

Mrs Weatherby walked towards the sink. There was something hesitant in her walk as if she was dreading what she might find. She put her hand on the handle of the top drawer.

'How many sets did you have there?' I asked.

'Two,' she said. 'I checked the other day.'

Having said that, she wasn't so keen to open the drawer. She moved as if in slow motion, as if she was dreading the outcome of her action. But finally she opened it. She looked in, and then took something out.

'One,' she said and held up a trio of keys on a silver ring. She put it on the surface and then she looked again. Carefully she picked up the paper napkins, the tinfoil, the plastic freezer bags that were lying in the drawer. She did not stop until she had emptied it.

She glanced up, an expression of relief on her face.

'The other's gone,' she said. 'Alicia must have taken it.' She smiled. 'Let's make ourselves more comfortable.' She walked to the door and I followed her. When we were both outside, she put her hand on the door handle. She shivered as she touched it.

'I never did like that room,' she said. 'I don't know why.'

She pulled the door shut.

125

Trevor Plastid was looking out of the window when we came back into the living room. He must have been in quite a reverie. When he heard us he jumped, turned and looked guiltily in our direction.

'We only found one set of keys,' Marion Weatherby said.

'Oh, good,' he said, puzzled, as if he, like me, could not quite understand the note of triumph in her voice.

She walked over to a cabinet.

'A brandy?' she offered.

Trevor refused at first but he changed his mind when I accepted. She got out a crystal decanter and poured each of us a healthy measure of a drink which had started as grapes some considerable time ago. We all sipped it appreciatively – it demanded at least that.

As the first drops of the velvety liquid rolled down my throat I put my glass down.

'What do you want from me?' I asked.

'Find Alicia,' Mrs Weatherby said. 'Bring her back.'

'Any idea where she went?'

The mother shook her head. 'I never interfered in her private life,' she said. 'To be honest, I always found it rather tedious.'

I got up. I saw Marion Weatherby's shocked look at my half-full glass and I almost told her I knew it was a crime to walk out on a brandy so good. But I didn't. If I had, I would have also had to tell her that suddenly I didn't want to be in her room, drinking in her largesse along with her brandy.

When I got outside Eva was waiting for me. She'd thrown a coat on top of her dressing-gown but even so she was shivering. Her breath came out foggy into the early morning light. She clapped her hands together.

'I thought you would never get here,' she said.

'Sorry,' I explained. 'Brandy. Too good to miss.'

She smiled. 'I know,' she said. 'I've tasted it.' She slipped one hand under my arm. 'Let me walk you to your car. I'll freeze if I have to stand much longer.'

126

I pointed us in the right direction and we walked along companionably, breathing in the crisp freshness of a day that had not yet been tainted by traffic fumes. Just before we reached my car, Eva spoke. 'Is she shouting blue Ming murder?'

'In a way,' I said. 'But she seems more concerned to have Alicia back.'

'Don't you believe it,' Eva said.

I looked at her inquisitively.

'Oh, she does want Alicia back,' she said. 'I don't think she'll ever allow that girl to slip through her fingers. No, what I mean is, don't believe the Ming story.'

'Why not?'

'I heard Marion get up this morning,' Eva said. 'I was in the kitchen, studying for my interpreter's test.'

'Chinese?'

'Yeah,' she said. 'An appropriate language somehow for three o'clock in the morning.'

'I'll take your word for it.'

'Anyway, I heard Marion. At first I ignored her. She often prowls about the place – she's got a bad case of insomnia – and so I didn't take any notice of her until I heard a shout and a crash. I went to investigate, making sure she didn't see me. I didn't want her to think I was spying on her late-night drinking bouts.'

'I get the picture,' I said.

'Except this wasn't one of them,' Eva said. 'When I looked in the living room I saw that she had broken an ashtray. It was in pieces by her feet, but she ignored it. She was standing by that spindly antique bureau she keeps by the window. Its lid was open and she was pulling papers out of it, searching for something. She was crying. I watched her for a bit. I knew better than to ask if she needed help. It took a long time but eventually she calmed herself down and looked like she'd made up her mind about something. She stuffed the papers back and shut the desk. Then she went to the phone and called the ghoul.'

'Plastid?'

Eva nodded. 'That's the one. Always hovering round her with his tongue hanging out. I could have told him not to bother, she's not interested. He's very persistent though.'

She frowned as if trying to work something out. 'Suppose he . . .' she started and then she shook her head. 'Not a solicitor,' she said.

'What did she say to him?'

'She asked him, instructed him, to get over right away. She said her Ming had gone missing and she was afraid that Alicia had taken it.'

'And so?' I asked.

'So nothing,' Eva said. 'Unless you think that there's something fishy in the fact that the Ming was in its usual place and that I watched her as she went up to it, took it down and hid it. It's under the lid of the grand piano.'

'Oh,' I managed.

'Quite right, madam detective,' Eva said. 'And now I'm off to bed.'

'Thanks,' I called as she hurried off.

She fluttered a hand in acknowledgment. I climbed into my car and drove off towards the pink glow of the dawn.

Eleven

I sat at my window and watched Dalston waking up to another day of struggle. It did so with an effort. Cold was etched into everything – the lips of the milkman as he inched his way down the road, the hunched shoulders of the paper boy as he wearily mounted one step after another, and the breath of the postman as he sent another series of bills on the last lap of their journey.

I had tried to use my time of watching to think out what to do but my mind kept flitting from one thing to another – from the corpse of James Morgan to his smile; from the letter left by Pete to his brooding presence; from the self-satisfied face of Gordon Jarvis to the wreck of Elmore's body; and, finally, from Alicia's frantic performances to her mother's icy stare.

Images of all these people swirled in my head but not in any constructive kind of way. I tried to console myself by telling myself that this was tiredness operating, but it didn't work; tired or not, I knew that I'd managed to collect the facts but somehow completely missed the pattern that might explain them. Not a very flattering observation for a detective to make about herself.

I might have continued in this vein if Carmen hadn't turned up. She let herself in with the spare key I'd once given her. She was singing as she did so. She came into the room still singing. Under her arm she carried some paper bags. She hadn't expected to find me awake and she looked startled when she saw me.

'Up already?' she said. 'Very impressive.'

She held up one bag. '*Pain chocolat*,' she said. She held up another. 'Croissant. I'll put the coffee on.'

While she busied herself in the kitchen I told her about my nocturnal visit. She whistled through her teeth.

We sat down and drank the coffee in bowls with some milk that Carmen had warmed. We dunked the pastries into the creamy combination. When we'd both got through our first bowl and were into our second, I spoke again.

'What brought you here so early?' I asked.

'Your engagements,' she said. 'You've got a busy day ahead. Two funerals and a widow to visit. Thought you might want company.'

I nodded my appreciation.

'Pete's as well?' I asked.

'Afraid so,' she said. 'His is first.'

'They're burying him indecently fast,' I said.

'Cremating,' she corrected.

'What about the post mortem?'

'It's done,' she said. 'I reckon we can pay a visit to the doctor in between cremation one and funeral two.'

'Yeugh,' I said.

'Doubled,' she answered.

Pete's funeral was a depressing affair. That may sound like an odd way to describe a funeral but, in my experience, funerals don't have to be depressing. Sad maybe, painful often, but not that overwhelming sense of defeat and inaction that comes from depression. Pete had behaved as if he'd never had a chance and the service they'd laid on for him reflected this.

A handful of people were dotted about in the small chapel that adjoined the crematorium. Family in the front row stared stoically ahead as the priest tried his best to say something appropriate about someone he had never met and wouldn't have understood if he had.

A few friends occupied the back row. They were a motley

crew. Some of them, with the unengaged eyes of drug-abusers, stared into the distance of their own fate – Pete's death reaching them but not quite getting to them. Alicia was not among them. Nor was she with the tiny band of youth that I'd seen after the St James's concert who looked thoroughly embarrassed to find themselves at such an event.

As soon as the ceremony was over, I made a bee-line for the music lovers. There were three of them: three sullen-looking teenagers who had tried to do the right thing and now wanted to run away back into the light of their own carefree worlds. They wanted to, but they didn't quite feel ready for it. Instead they hung around the exit, waiting for the family to leave and trying to keep their faces in suitable funereal poses.

I approached them.

'You're friends of Alicia's, aren't you?' I said.

The two boys kept their eyes on their polished shoes. The girl nodded.

'Do you know where she is?' I asked.

All three shook their heads in unison.

'How did you know about the funeral?'

The girl looked me in the eye. 'We heard about it,' she said.

They had the stubbornness of youth confronted by an authority that they could defy without losing face. I wasn't going to get anywhere with them, and I knew it.

'Give Alicia a message from me,' I said. 'Tell her, Kate's looking for her. Tell her I want to help. Say that I won't tell her mother without her consent.'

One of the boys spoke for the first time. 'What makes you think we'll see her?' he said loudly in a voice whose arrogance made me bristle. The girl didn't say anything. She nodded, almost imperceptibly, but it was a nod.

I walked away from them. Carmen had been standing by the wreaths and she called my attention to them. She was pointing at one in particular – a small delicate collection of roses intertwined to make a heart shape. I knelt down and read the inscription on the card. 'To Pete,' it said. 'In death shall we be united. A.'

I looked up at Carmen. 'We better find her quick,' I said.

'That's for sure,' she said.

We were halfway out of the place when a young man blocked my exit. He was misshapen and stooped. He held his body as if willing it to disappear. He avoided my gaze. He sniffed.

'You're the person who's been asking questions,' he said in a dull voice.

'Yes.'

'You have anything to do with the police?' he asked.

'Nothing at all.'

'Why are you interested in Pete's death?'

'I have my reasons. Do you want to tell me something?'

A sly look came over his face. For the first time he stared straight at me, assessing me.

'What's it worth?'

I shifted my weight to the right. I started to move round him. He was after money, I could tell that, but I didn't know if he had anything to sell.

'Not much,' I said and got ready to leave.

He sniffed again and shifted with me.

'A tenner,' he said.

A tenner seemed cheap for information and recoverable without it. What did I have to lose? I nodded.

He shoved his hand in front of me. I put two five-pound notes into it. He had a funny look in his eyes and so I kept my arm resting on his. Just in case he tried to walk off.

'Pete never snuffed himself,' he said.

'How do you know?'

'Because his gear was with him,' he said. 'And there was some scag in it. A lot.'

'How do you know?' I asked.

He shook his head. 'I got told.'

'And if it's true,' I said, 'why does that mean that he didn't kill himself?'

He looked at me as if I were mad, as if I were so naive that he couldn't believe that I still functioned in the world.

'It stands to reason,' he said. 'If he were going to off himself he would have taken the lot. He'd just scored. He had a lot of stuff on him. Why leave it behind?' He nodded to himself as if confirming one of the undying rules of life. 'He would have taken the lot,' he repeated.

I kept my hand on his wrist at the same time as I flicked my eyes towards Carmen. She understood immediately. She moved in close. The boy didn't see her doing it but he sensed that something was up. He looked uneasy and his right eyelid began to pulse nervously.

'I told you what I know,' he said.

'But not where you got your information from.'

The eyelid went again. He tried not to show that he was looking around him, assessing his exit point. I didn't mind. It gave him the chance to see Carmen standing there.

'I can't tell you,' he said.

I reached into my bag and took out another fiver. I held it towards him.

'How do you know Pete had more heroin on him?' I asked.

'He told me,' the youth said, without taking his eyes off the money. 'I tried to score off him earlier that day. Pete had good contacts – he knew where to lay his hands on the stuff and it was always the best. I saw him that morning and he didn't have nothing. He was waiting for his man. That's what he told me. He didn't have enough even for himself. He told me to come back later.'

'Maybe his dealer didn't turn up,' I said. I rustled the money and watched his eyes follow it.

'He did,' the boy said.

'How do you know?' I repeated.

'I waited outside the flat he was staying in. I had nowhere else to go and I was, you know, desperate. I saw the man go in and then come out.'

'And then?'

133

'I waited some more,' he said. 'Pete could turn nasty if you pushed him. I gave him time to get his own thing together. Then I went upstairs.'

'And?'

'I couldn't get in,' he said. 'The door was locked.'

He said it quickly and without conviction. He couldn't keep his body still while he said it, nor his voice on an even keel.

'You saw him dead,' I said. He didn't respond.

'And you took the dope,' I finished.

This time alarm crossed his face. I realised it was the first emotion I'd seen on it.

'I never,' he protested. 'I never did. I was scared. I got out of there. I ran away. I never took nothing.'

'Who was his dealer?' I asked.

His face went blank again.

'Who was it?' I repeated.

He shook his head. I looked at Carmen. She shrugged. I held the money out to him. He grabbed it.

He turned to go. As he did he must have seen something in my face; some flash of pity or some remnant of contempt. He stopped.

'I liked Pete,' he said. 'If there was anything I could have done to save him I would have. But he was stone cold.'

'But you can help me now,' I said. 'Tell me who his dealer was.'

'I don't know his name,' he replied. 'I only saw him pass by quickly. He was a private contact of Pete's. A big dealer who liked to operate on his own – no middle man. Pete said he was a weirdo who got his kicks from dealing. From another world, he said.'

'What did he mean – another world?'

'I dunno. Pete talked in riddles sometimes.'

The boy's eyes misted over. He turned again and this time he walked away without pausing. We watched him go.

'Do you believe him?' Carmen asked.

'Some of it,' I said. 'But even if what he says is true, that

134

doesn't mean Pete was murdered. He could have left some dope.'

I heard my voice as I said it. Even to me, it sounded hollow.

Carmen drove while I looked out for a telephone box. Eventually I found one. She stopped and waited. I went in and dialled. He answered on the second ring in a calm, slow, sleepy way.

'Toby?'

'Kate,' he said. 'How charming.'

There was a crackling sound as he transferred the receiver from one ear to the other. I thought I heard somebody mutter beside him.

'I need your help,' I said.

'For you, anything,' he answered.

'I've got to find Alicia,' I said.

There was silence at the other end.

'Alicia Weatherby,' I said.

His voice had lost some of its charm when he spoke again.

'I know who you mean,' he drawled. 'How utterly disappointing. I thought that it was for my body that you phoned.'

'It's important,' I said.

'So I gather,' he said drily.

'Will you help?'

'Why am I so obliging?' he said, as if to himself.

'That means yes?'

'If you'll meet me later,' he said.

I agreed and I took down the address he gave me. I hung up without saying goodbye.

Charles Kirby was waiting for us, leaning by a coffee machine in a corridor of what looked more like a factory than a hospital. He was dressed in doctor white and he sported doctor anxiety but he let his frown leave for a second when he saw Carmen. He came towards us, his body unfolding as

135

he did so until he had stretched to his full six foot five. He grabbed Carmen and engulfed her in a huge embrace. She returned the hug with good measure. Her face reached his armpit. I tossed a silent question in her direction.

'I have friends in all the best places,' she said. 'You name them. Pubs . . . clubs . . . mortuaries.'

Charles laughed and let go of her. He turned to me.

'You must be Kate,' he said. 'Carmen told me about you. Let's go somewhere more private.'

He led us down the maze of hospital corridors with their pea-green walls and intimations of disease. He stopped when he came to an unmarked door. He took out a key and opened it. He gestured for us to go in.

The room was small, if you could call it a room. It didn't really qualify as one. It was more in the nature of a cupboard, a neatly labelled cupboard, but a cupboard nevertheless.

'Charles,' Carmen protested. 'Your anti-social habits are getting beyond a joke.'

'You don't know the type of company I have to endure in the doctors' common room,' he said. 'This place might be cramped but at least it's not haunted by pompous thirty-year-olds whose prime aim is to arse-lick their way into consultancies.'

He gestured to a shelf that had nothing above it.

'Take a seat,' he said. 'That way we won't use up all the oxygen at once.'

Carmen and I sat while he remained where he was, towering above us.

Charles had noticed my confusion right away and he set about clearing it up.

'Carmen and I are old friends,' he said. 'We met at a medical convention.'

'Oh,' I said.

He laughed. 'An eminent consultant, my ex-professor in fact, was giving a talk on sickle-cell anaemia and Carmen and her friends intervened.'

'Disrupted, you mean,' Carmen said.

'Well there was that element,' he said. 'I, for one, found it most instructive. I sought out her company afterwards.'

'He bailed me out,' Carmen explained.

'And heartily pleased I have always been that I did. Carmen's friendship has given me much pleasure. And interest.'

His upper-class voice reverberated round the small room. Once again, I reflected on how little I actually knew about Carmen.

He looked at his watch.

'What can I do for you?' he asked.

'Did you do the post mortem on Pete Archie?' Carmen said.

He shook his head. 'No,' he said. 'But after you phoned I glanced at the report.'

'And?'

'Inhalation pneumonia followed by cardiac arrest. He died of a drug overdose,' he explained when he noticed my confusion. 'But the actual mechanism of his death, the reason his body stopped functioning, was that he inhaled his own vomit and asphyxiated.'

'Is that usual?' Carmen said.

He screwed up his face for a moment. 'Well . . .' he said, doubtfully.

'Come on, Charles,' Carmen urged. 'Take a risk. Give us your honest opinion.'

He wasn't rattled by the impatience in her voice. He smiled.

'Hard to throw off the mantle of professional caution,' he said. 'but here goes. I don't know how much you know about drug-related deaths?'

He paused for our response.

'Assume ignorance,' Carmen said.

'Well,' he said, 'contrary to popular opinion, heroin addicts don't usually die from an overdose of the pure drug. It doesn't rush to their hearts and kill them, especially not in these days of unscrupulous salesmen. You see, the heroin now available for sale is not pure – nowhere near pure in fact. It's cut with all kinds of substances – sugar, flour, talcum powder, anything that won't be easily detected. And that's where the trouble starts. Because when heroin is cut with other substances – substances which are innocuous on their own – it can be fatal. They can get stuck, if you like, in the veins, causing temporary hiccups, haemorrhages and eventual death. Your friend died like that. That fact in itself is not out of the ordinary.'

'So what worries you?' Carmen asked.

'It's just a feeling,' Charles said.

We both nodded.

'Perhaps I wouldn't have been so hasty with the death certificate if I had been in charge,' he continued. 'You see, Pete's blood was contaminated by a very unusual additive – a potassium compound usually only available on prescription. We don't often see it, and I've never before heard of it being implicated in an overdose. I cannot imagine that your street dealer would be cutting his heroin with it.'

'But your colleague disagrees?' Carmen asked.

He shrugged his massive shoulders.

'It's unfortunate,' he said, 'but heroin deaths have reached epidemic proportions. One can become careless about PMS. Plus there is a tendency on the part of the medical establishment to regard addicts as less, shall we say, worthy of attention. Especially dead addicts.'

'Who would have access to this contaminant?' I asked.

'In this country, very few people,' he said. 'It has long been withdrawn. But in other places which are less careful about their drug control, you could probably buy it over the counter. Which, I suppose, would fit if the heroin was cut before entering the country. A possibility, I suppose, although unusual since smugglers do their damnedest to keep down the bulk of their imports.'

He thought about what he'd just said. 'I cannot be sure without further investigation. All I can tell you is that if I had done the PM there would have been some doubt in my mind: some cause for exploration if only to try and prevent further tragedies of this kind.'

At that moment there was a sharp bleeping noise from his top pocket. He reached into it and pulled out a pager. He flicked a switch and it stopped making a noise.

'Must dash,' he said apologetically.

'Thanks,' I said.

He dismissed my gratitude with a flick of his hand. 'Any time,' he said. 'For a friend of Carmen's.'

He let us out of the cupboard and locked it. He shook hands with us before he sloped off.

We walked towards the exit.

'You know what this means,' I said, just as we reached it. 'Pete was murdered.'

Carmen had her hand on one of the swing doors. She looked at me without moving. 'But then you always knew that,' she said. She pushed at the door and it opened wide to let us out.

It took us some time to reach our second funeral of the day. James Morgan had family in the country and he was to be buried in a Hertfordshire cemetery overlooking rolling hills. The service was held in an old church nearby. Carmen and I reached it just as the opening crescendo of organ music had swelled and was hovering in the air. We seated ourselves at the back.

The contrast between this gathering and the last made the waste of Pete's life even more acute. James Morgan's death, like Pete's, was a tragedy of a life cut short. But the difference between the two ceremonies was that at Morgan's burial there was a testimony to the kind of man he had been. For a start the presiding vicar had either known Morgan or had been properly briefed; there was none of that awkwardness of trying to describe, in Christian terms, the life of someone who might never have existed. Instead we had a eulogy about Morgan's work sprinkled with references, jokes and anecdotes which made Morgan a person rather than a function. On top of that we heard a selection of poems – a bit of Blake, a touch of Keats – all read by people who had no trouble projecting their voices. And finally, there was, of course, the organ music – played by a succession of young people, some of whom had great difficulty restraining their tears. The music swelled up, filling the airy church with splendour.

The congregation filed out to the sound of Bach. Carmen and I remained seated as the people from the front pews left first. There was a group that was obviously family, including a frail woman leaning on two sticks who looked numb with pain. I guessed she was Morgan's mother. On each side of her was a man hovering close enough to catch her if she fell. They must have been Morgan's brothers. They in turn were followed by two smartly dressed women who must have been their wives. There was no indication, in that first family group, of any person who had been tied to Morgan other than by blood.

There were close friends, though. They had been sitting in the second row and the rest of the congregation included them in the family group by waiting for them to leave. There were six of them and they all walked past slowly, each lost in grief. They were a well-dressed and respectable lot but their respectability was tinged with something more flamboyant than the sober appearance of Morgan's family. It wasn't so much in the colour of their clothes, since they had all restricted themselves to the conventions of funereal dark, but more in the way they carried themselves.

There was one man among them who seemed different. He had all the assurance of the others but his manner was a touch more conservative and his dress a mite more conventional. And yet he did not look ordinary. His skin was tanned and weather-beaten. He had strong features, bright blue eyes and a broad forehead, all of which made him seem impressive. There was something un-English about the way he carried himself; something that indicated that he had lived

140

outside the sanctuary of the British ruling class.

He passed by. Carmen and I remained where we were until the rest of the congregation had filed out. There were plenty of them, and it took some time. When it got to our turn we stepped into the cold of the fading afternoon light to the accompaniment of revving motor cars. We got into my car and followed the procession to the cemetery.

The burial itself was an anti-climax. We gathered round the grave and watched the coffin being lowered into it. I thought, as I always do at English funerals, that, after the religion is over, the body is disposed of with unseemly haste. There was just time for Morgan's mother to look briefly into the hole, to shake off the arm of one of her sons and to mutter something, something bitter about the unfairness of it all, before the congregation turned away. Frantic chat took the place of self-imposed gravity.

Carmen and I moved towards the back of the crowd where the younger contingent had gathered. Relief that the ceremony was over had given the group a kind of carnival air and it wasn't hard to strike up a conversation. I approached one of the young women who had played in the church. She was small in stature but had a kind of rotundity that gave her presence. She carried herself straight and poised as if years on the music circuit had given her confidence beyond her age. Her cheeks were still smeared with the tears that she hadn't bothered to conceal. I thought I had detected anger in her playing and when I looked at her face I saw that it was hardened by something more permanent than her grief; by something soured and unsatisfied.

'Did you know James long?' I asked.

She shook her head. 'Not really. I was a recent addition to his stable. But he saved my life.'

'Did he often rescue people in trouble?'

She paused before answering. A grimace crossed her face and showed that she didn't like to be thought of as vulnerable, despite what she had said. 'He went for people with talent,' she explained in an exasperated voice. 'When I said that he saved my life I suppose what I meant was that he rescued my career when it was in a trough.' She looked up at me from her five foot no inches and continued, 'My career is my life. I am music and music is me.'

It sounded a bit like a litany and I wondered whether it was one that James Morgan had taught her. Not for the first time I tried to work out what had been in it for James. It's one thing to get vicarious pleasure from helping people achieve what you can no longer do – that I could understand. But if Alicia Weatherby, and now this girl, were anything to go by, James Morgan had chosen the most difficult personalities to nurture.

'Do you know Alicia Weatherby?' I asked.

The girl frowned with distaste. 'I've met her,' she said briskly.

'You didn't approve?'

'I wouldn't have chosen to work with her,' she said. 'But I wasn't James' keeper.'

She implied that she should have been. I kept silent, hoping she would feel the need to fill the gap. I was in luck.

'I don't understand what he saw in her,' she said. 'Oh, I admit that Alicia has talent. But it's a kind of fly-by-night talent: unformed and untameable. She can play with genius but genius is so unpredictable, don't you think?'

Again I didn't speak, so she had to answer herself.

'In my opinion, Alicia is going to burn out soon. I said as much to James but he was obsessed by Alicia. He couldn't keep away from her.'

'Was it a long obsession?'

She laughed patronisingly. 'James was always a quick mover,' she said. 'His more outrageous whims came to him suddenly.'

She saw somebody in the distance who was waving to her. She waved back. She gave me a crisp, cold smile. 'Nice to talk to you,' she said and then she walked off.

'Uh uh, jealousy,' Carmen said in my ear.

'Rampant,' I said. 'Not a healthy world they move in.'

Carmen, who had been scanning the crowd while we talked, froze suddenly. She gripped my arm.

'Well, well, well,' she said. She nodded her head in the direction of a group of people standing by Morgan's grave. 'Look who's there.'

I looked but I didn't see anything to take my breath away. I glanced back at Carmen, puzzled.

'Not there,' Carmen said. 'To the right.'

I looked again. And saw them: the man I'd noticed coming out of the church engaged in deep conversation with Marion Weatherby. They looked as if they were arguing.

'This is a case for super-sleuth,' Carmen said. 'Meet you at the gates.' She pushed me towards Marion.

I tried to sneak up on them but I hadn't reckoned on Marion's nervous energy. Despite the fact that she was listening attentively to the man, she had one eye open to movements around her. She saw me coming. A look of alarm crossed her face. She said something to the man who also glanced up. He threw me a dirty look before walking off briskly.

Marion intercepted me in case I was going to follow him.

'Found Alicia?' she asked.

'No. What brings you here?'

'Paying my respects,' she said. 'After all, James Morgan made a very generous offer to Alicia. And we are implicated in his death.'

'That's one way of putting it,' I said.

'Put it any way you want,' she said. 'Just find my daughter. Fast.'

'Try helping me then,' I said.

'I've told you all I know,' she said. 'What could I possibly be concealing?'

'Looked in the piano recently?' I asked.

She froze with indignation. 'How dare you search my flat?' she snapped. 'Who asked you to pry?'

Before I could come up with a suitably smart-aleck reply she turned and walked rapidly away.

Carmen was waiting patiently for me by the wrought-iron gates at the entrance.

'I hereby give up all claims to super-sleuth status,' I said. 'I've just found out nothing with a capital N.'

Carmen smiled sweetly. 'Lucky I'm with you then,' she said in an infuriatingly self-satisfied manner.

'Yes?'

'Guess who the man we saw talking to Marion is?'

I threw up my hands in impatience. 'Haven't got a clue.'

Carmen pouted. 'You're no fun.'

She saw the thunder in my face. 'Okay, okay, I'll tell you,' she said. 'And don't say it wasn't worth waiting for. That man was once James Morgan's best friend.'

'So?'

'That's not all he is. He's also Marion Weatherby's ex-husband – the elusive Richard Weatherby.'

I opened my mouth and then closed it again.

'What did I tell you?' she asked.

'It was worth waiting for,' I agreed. 'I have no idea what it means, but it sure was worth waiting for.'

She grinned. 'Let's go,' she said. 'Before everybody has the same idea and we get caught in a traffic jam all the way to SW1.'

We walked to the car. On the way we passed a familiar face, sitting in a powder-blue BMW.

'That man goes beyond the call of duty,' I commented.

'Who is it?' Carmen asked.

'Trevor Plastid. Weatherby solicitor-cum-chauffeur, it looks like.'

We got into the car. Only as I was driving off did I return to Carmen's revelation.

'What do you mean he was "once" Morgan's best friend?' I asked.

'Couldn't get it out of my source,' Carmen replied. 'But Richard and James hadn't been seen together for years. My source didn't even know that Richard was still around.'

'As a matter of interest, who was your source?'

'Morgan's mother,' Carmen said. 'Nobody else seemed to want to talk to her. Probably felt too embarrassed at her grief.'

I stared at Carmen in admiration.

'You're quite a woman,' I said.

'Keep your eyes on the road,' she replied.

Twelve

We got back into town at six o'clock and suffered the consequences. The streets were packed with irate drivers all trying to pretend that their working day was over and that they were free. Which was unfortunate, given that they were stuck in the same traffic jams as us and were acting as if every car ahead of them was personally blighting their lives and every car behind was a potential threat.

In the muddle we made slow progress and it was seven before we arrived at Mare Street. We negotiated the one-way system round Victoria Park and eventually drew up outside a dilapidated three-storey house. Somebody had made an attempt to give it a lift by painting the front door poster-red but they'd reckoned without the elements, and the paint was peeling off to reveal the sludge brown underneath. The rest of the street was just as run down: it had gone through a phase of genteel decay and was now headed for full-scale deterioration. It was ironic, considering that, two blocks down in the area bordering Victoria Park, you could just about buy a one-room bedsit if you had £50,000 to spare. But in this street the houses were a shade too small, and a few too many yards away from tube or park to merit major rejuvenation.

As instructed by Elmore we rang the middle of the three bells, and waited.

It was a while before we got any response. Finally there was the sound of light feet on the stairs and the sight, through the frosted glass, of a small hand reaching up to get at the door catch. The hand succeeded after a bit of straining and the door opened slowly.

She was about four years old and cute with it. Large blue eyes set in a chubby face looked at us seriously.

'Yes?' she piped.

'Is your mummy in?' Carmen asked gently.

The little girl nodded.

'She's upstairs with Danny,' she said. 'My daddy isn't there. He's died.'

She looked at us to see if we understood.

'He's never coming back,' she explained.

A woman's voice shouted from the stairwell. 'Who is it, Meg?'

'Ladies,' the girl said.

The woman appeared from around the bend on the first floor. She looked like her little girl but without the brightness or the energy. She was tired and harassed and her back was bent with the strain of carrying the toddler under her right arm. With her left hand she swept away a strand of mouse-coloured hair that had fallen over her face.

'Can I help you?' she asked in a voice which was on the verge of cracking.

'Elmore sent us,' Carmen said. 'It's about Mately's.'

The woman sighed loudly.

'You better come in,' she said. She walked slowly up the stairs.

Guided by the little girl we followed. We were shown into a small flat on the second floor. A tiny entrance hall led into a sitting room that wasn't much bigger, and which was further diminished by the old-fashioned furniture that was crammed into it. The woman was at the table, stuffing food into her youngest child's disinterested mouth.

'Excuse the mess,' she said automatically.

We introduced ourselves and she nodded at us.

'And I'm Sarah Parsons,' she said, 'Tommy's wife. But then you know that.'

We both offered her our condolences which she accepted as if she'd got used to accepting them. Her toddler squalled at the withdrawal of her attention and she went back to filling him up.

'We've come at a bad time,' I observed.

'Any time's bad,' she said. 'When you're alone with kids.'

She must have heard how the echo of that sentence sounded because she smiled apologetically.

'Even when Tommy was alive, it was hell between six and eight, what with them fractious and us hungry.'

'What's fractious?' Meg asked.

'Irritable,' her mother said. She looked at us. 'I told Elmore he was wasting your time,' she said. 'I'm not opening it all up again. I'm satisfied with my deal.'

'What did they give you?' Carmen asked.

'Ten thousand quid,' she said.

Ten thousand pounds, I thought, for a man's life. Carmen must have thought the same. We glanced at each other. Sarah Parsons intercepted the look.

'I know what you're thinking,' she said. 'But it's not your choice, is it? It's not you that's left with two live children and a dead hero. It's not you that would have to take them to court and maybe lose everything. So it's not for you to judge, is it?'

As if picking up the bitterness in her voice, the toddler began to cry. She registered the noise. Automatically, and without looking at him, she speeded up the pace of the spoonfuls of food. He shut his mouth to the onslaught and the food spattered on to her. She yanked at the bib around his neck and wiped him roughly with it. He went red. He opened his mouth again and he bawled.

She turned back to us. 'And what's Elmore playing at?' she said. 'He's okay. He's alive. It's my Tommy that suffered.'

She turned again to face her yelling infant. She picked him out of his high chair and jiggled him up and down. His yells increased.

There was not much we could do. We said goodbye and she nodded. She didn't choose to speak again. We left the room.

As we were about to go out the front door, a small voice from on high stopped us.

'I'm not,' Meg said, 'not flackshit. I never have been. And I'm not the other thing neither.'

Her face withdrew and I heard the sound of a door shutting.

Carmen and I didn't have much to say to each other about the visit. I felt bad about it and I was sure she did too but there were no words that would wipe out the memory of Sarah Parsons' desolation. I dropped Carmen at Highbury and Islington tube. Then I carried on towards my next destination.

On the way I stopped at a phone box. I dialled Sam's number. He sounded relieved to hear from me.

'Wondered where you were,' he said. 'I even went over to your flat in case you'd slept the whole day and left your answerphone on.'

'It's been a day of death,' I said, 'or the final result of it. I'll tell you later.'

'You're not coming home?' he asked almost plaintively.

I dealt with his disappointment by being flippant.

'Got a date,' I said. 'With my teenager admirer.'

'Oh.'

'You're not jealous are you?' I asked.

'Should I be?' Sam countered.

'No,' I said. 'This is business.'

'Well then, I hope it goes well,' he said. 'And by the way, your friend Jonathan Blenter has been trying to get hold of you. Talk about lugubrious – the telephone nearly slid down my throat when I was listening to him.'

'Did he say anything special?'

'Only that he found one of Gordon Jarvis' clients who wouldn't mind putting the boot in. He, the client, lost a lot of money over the fire while Jarvis was waiting for the insurance to turn up. So if there's any scandal the client would like a first bid on suing. Might be a way of getting Jarvis without dragging Elmore into it.'

'Sounds good,' I said. 'Specially after where I've just been. Why do I always have to be surprised to find that capitalists have less scruples than others?'

'I don't know, honey,' he said. 'Come home and we can explore the question.'

'Later,' I said.

'Well keep yourself fresh for me,' he said before hanging up.

I drove to north-west London on automatic. I concentrated so little on where I was going that I passed Toby's house altogether. Instead of doing a U-turn I drove into a side street and parked before walking the hundred yards back.

I was surprised when I reached Toby's flat. I shouldn't have been – I ought to have been warned by the Primrose Hill location and by the Maserati. But even these didn't alert me properly and I wondered why. I realised that my surprise was something to do with an old-fashioned concept of age. I hadn't associated such a degree of wealth with the under twenty-fives. Well, you live and learn.

Toby smiled, delighted and expectant, when he opened the door. He was wearing a pair of baggy fawn trousers which hung elegantly on his slim frame, and a matching fawn V-neck cashmere sweater. He showed me into an open-plan living room, architect-designed on three split levels, modern without being barren, opulent without being overstated. I whistled.

'Do you work for a living?' I asked.

'Would you like me to?' he answered.

He took my coat from my back in one smooth motion. I found myself speculating on whether he was as adept at removing other items of clothing.

He was gone from the room for a fraction of a second.

When he returned he was holding an ice bucket. There was a bottle sticking out of it. He tipped it in my direction, questioningly. It was a bottle of Bollinger. I nodded.

'Champagne's a drink to be enjoyed in private. Don't you agree?'

I can't say I had an answer for that one so I was relieved when he didn't wait for it. He popped the cork without fuss. He poured some of the liquid into two long-stemmed glasses and brought mine to me. He sat opposite. He raised his own glass in a silent salute.

For a time we sipped in a glow of trivial conversation. Toby steered the talk away from Alicia Weatherby and I let him do it. It had been a tiring day and the champagne was taking effect. I was happy to let him make the running while I enjoyed feeling the tension flow away.

It was some time before I got restless. When I did, he picked up the symptoms almost as soon as I did.

'I thought you might be hungry,' he said. 'I fixed us something simple.'

Something simple turned out to be something very expensive. We started with caviar – Russian baluga caviar – and we moved on to salmon – fresh salmon lightly cooked and accompanied by a salad of different shaped and coloured leaves. To finish we had water ice, yellow in colour and fragrant in taste.

'My compliments to your cook,' I said.

'How disappointing,' he said. 'And I was hoping you'd assume I'd made the meal. However, I will make you some coffee now.'

When he came back into the room he was carrying a tray. On it were two small coffee cups, a full percolator and two brandy glasses. He reached into a small cabinet on the wall and brought out a bottle of brandy. He poured me one without asking. It was the first mistake he'd made all evening.

Again he sat opposite me. While I had coffee he cupped his brandy glass between his hands, swirling it. Then he took a sip and put it down. He leaned forward.

'Kate,' he started.

'Toby,' I said in what I hoped was a reflection of his tone. He sat back, exasperated.

'Do you have to knock me off my stride?' he asked.

'Merely trying to save your energy,' I said.

He smiled, a charming seductive smile. He looked at his right index finger, licked it and then ran it teasingly along his lips.

'Don't you ever feel tempted to break the rules?' he asked. 'I'm attracted to you because of our differences. I'm not offering long-term commitment – just bliss.'

'You're confident,' I said.

He leaned forward again and before I could move out of his way he had taken one of my hands in his. He turned it palm upwards. He stroked it before lifting it to his mouth. He kissed it gently before returning it to me.

I felt a shiver run down my spine.

'Alicia Weatherby,' I said.

'You're incorrigible,' he said.

'I know,' I said. 'I have tried to warn you. Do you know where she is?'

'What would you give me if I told you?' he asked.

'My thanks,' I said. 'Do you know?'

He shrugged. 'Afraid not,' he said. 'I don't keep tabs on her any more.'

'Meaning that you used to?'

Again he shrugged. He was trying to impress without being caught out in the attempt.

'We had a thing,' he said. 'Didn't last long. She bored me.'

I didn't like his tone of voice. There was something hard in it, something a touch callous.

'She was too prim,' he continued. 'Not free in herself, if you know what I mean.'

'I can guess,' I said.

He picked up his brandy glass and held it to his mouth. He put his neck back and tossed the contents down his throat.

'What's up?' he asked. 'Do you disapprove of what I'm saying?'

'Should I?' I countered.

'Are you some kind of feminist?'

'Yes,' I said, 'without the some kind of.'

'I might have known,' he said to himself. His next remark was addressed to me. 'But I do so like a challenge.'

'Is that what's going on now?' I asked. 'A battle?'

'It takes two, you know,' he said. He smiled alluringly.

It was going on too long, this seduction scene. It was beginning to get on my nerves. 'Hey, Toby,' I tried. 'You don't have to make a conquest of every woman you like.'

'And what makes you assume I like you?' he asked.

I gave him one last try. 'Come on, Toby,' I said.

He chose to ignore the tension in my voice. 'Is that an invitation?' he quipped.

'Forget it,' I said. I stood up.

He didn't like that. He sneered at me. 'Your type stick together,' he said. 'You girls think you can walk all over men.'

'Actually I was planning to walk around you,' I answered.

'Ha, ha. You think you're smart. Well, lady, let me tell you one thing. Your friend Alicia was well and truly fucked up. Ask anybody who tried her. Flirt wasn't in it, but get her in the bedroom, and she turned into a twelve-year-old. Might turn some chaps on but I can't say that I'm into paedophilia.'

Oh shit, I thought, I didn't know it was going to be this bad. I'd assumed that underneath the childish manoeuvring lurked somebody who liked women. Obviously I was wrong. I'd been misled by the elegant clothes and the smooth manner. There was nothing attractive about Toby any more – all he projected was a deep-rooted hatred. I felt cross with myself for ever flirting with the idea – even if only in fantasy – of letting things get out of hand.

I walked out of the room. I got my coat from the cupboard in the hall and marched to the front door. He was watching me. I snatched a quick glance at his face. I thought he was

153

looking a trifle ashamed of himself but I no longer trusted my perceptions in relation to him.

'Let's not part like this,' he said. He gestured to show he meant me no harm.

'Grow up,' I said. I walked out. I shut the door firmly behind me.

The cold hit me as I stepped outside. I sobered up immediately. It was a dark night but I didn't mind that. I was relieved to have got away from Toby.

I walked briskly back to my car, breathing in the night air. The roads were deserted. I was wearing sneakers and I padded past the parked cars and palatial houses without a sound. The silence had a strange effect. My ears felt muffled as if I was recovering from a dose of overloud music. I trod through the silence, my thoughts on home, bed and Sam.

It was only when I was a stone's throw from my car that I sensed something amiss. I didn't hear anything, but I began to suspect that I was being followed: somebody was moving stealthily and deliberately towards me.

I stopped myself from looking back. I kept moving while a cold fear grew inside me. At first I told myself that I was being over-cautious. I slowed down, telling myself that whoever was following would soon pass. But when they didn't, when their footsteps stopped with mine, I knew I was in trouble. I started to walk again – more briskly this time.

Everything sharpened into focus. My surroundings took on a kind of nightmare quality. The houses seemed to have taken a step backwards – the safety of their front doors was miles away. I tried again to convince myself that I was imagining things, that there was nobody creeping up behind, but a faint creak cut through my attempts to reassure myself.

I felt a rush of adrenalin and then an icy calm. I reached into my bag and took out my keys. Only then did I increase my pace. I tried to keep the acceleration as natural-looking as possible but I could hear the gasps of my own fear, and I was certain that whoever was following could hear them too.

He toyed with me. I realised that later. At any one moment he could have overtaken me but he chose not to. Instead he allowed the closeness of my car to tantalise me, he let me feel safe before making his move.

I had the key in the lock when I was grabbed from behind. A man's hand covered my mouth, another hand closed round my waist.

'Interfering cunt,' a voice whispered. 'When I'm finished with you you'll wish you'd kept out of other people's business.'

At his first contact I was overwhelmed by a wave of panic. It didn't last long. It was rapidly replaced by a feeling of acceptance – acceptance that this was actually happening to me, combined with a fear that I might not come out of it alive.

The acceptance brought a kind of relaxation. Scared as I was, some part of my brain kept on functioning. It did more than that – it functioned at a speed I'd not have thought possible and began working out odds: what if I fought back? What was he after? Was it better to pretend I'd given in? Could I make a run for it? And then almost simultaneously it came up with conclusions. I use the word it because that's what it felt like. To disassociate myself from the fear I had split myself in two.

The rational part told me to bite his hand. I bit his hand. It told me to scream when he released his hand momentarily. I screamed. It told me that if I kept struggling after his hand clamped back I might suffocate. I stopped struggling and was wrestled to the floor. It told me to breathe with his blows as he kicked me, first in the chest and then in the stomach. I breathed and sobbed with the pain of it. The man, a dark shadow looming above me with a cap pulled low over his face, looked down from a height and smiled.

'Mately's sends its compliments,' he said.

He took a step back and lifted his leg to kick me again. I cringed and then once again waited, eyes closed for the blow.

It was a blow that never came. Instead I heard the sound of

running feet, and the shouts of aristocratic outrage. I breathed out. I waited motionless.

The next thing I felt was a hand on me. I shrank away from it. It was removed.

'Kate,' I heard Toby say, 'are you all right?'

Still I didn't open my eyes. 'Is he gone?'

'He ran off. Are you all right?'

I opened my eyes. I was hit by a wave of nausea that could have been relief but felt like death.

'What does it look like?' I snapped. 'I'm obviously not all right.'

Toby smiled. It seemed like an odd response but I guess he was just relieved that I'd opened my eyes.

'I came after you to apologise,' he said. 'My behaviour was deplorable.'

'Thank God you were well brought up,' I said. 'But did you have to wait so long?'

'I hesitated,' he said. 'I thought you might not want to see me.'

'How times change,' I said. 'Help me up, will you?'

He reached over and pulled at me. An agonising pain crossed my chest. I screamed.

He stepped back. 'I'll go and call an ambulance,' he said.

I grasped his leg. 'Don't leave me,' I said quickly.

'But Kate, you're injured,' he said.

'Don't leave me,' I repeated.

I had managed to keep pretty calm until then but, hearing the desperation in my voice, I realised the shock I'd experienced. I began to weep, long shaking sobs that hurt but which also brought their own relief. Toby sat beside me, while I wept.

When the tears stopped flowing I felt a thousand times better in spirit and a lot worse in body. 'I think I've broken a rib,' I said. 'It's happened before. It's very painful but not dangerous. Help me up.'

This time I bit back the scream when he lifted me. I survived the lift just like I survived the walk to his flat. When

156

he had put me down on a couch, he looked a question at me.

'Ring Sam,' I said.

'The boyfriend, I assume,' he said. I nodded.

The rest of the evening was a big blur. Sam arrived, took one look at me and went into action. While I lay dazed a doctor prodded at me, an ambulance transported me, an X-ray machine hummed over me, and the police questioned me. The police went away with vows to do their best to catch my assailant; I didn't tell them about Mately's, and I guessed my case would soon be shelved. The medical department were more specific. My stomach, they said, was okay but bruised. The only damage to my body was two broken ribs.

They wouldn't let me go home. They hospitalised me for the night – just to be on the safe side, they said. I was beyond caring. Pain-killers and exhaustion meant that I kept slipping in and out of consciousness. I closed my eyes while I was wheeled on a trolley. The next thing I knew it was six-thirty in the morning and a white starched nurse was handing me a cup of tea.

I groaned and turned over. That was a mistake. I gave a yelp.

'Got to be more careful than that,' she said, cheerfully.

'Get me out of here,' I said.

Sam did. Six hours later.

Carmen came over late that afternoon. She looked at me and she didn't waste her breath asking for a bulletin. I guessed that anybody with their eyes in the right place could see how I felt. I reached for a pain-killer.

Sam moved the bottle out of my grasp.

'Afraid not,' he said. 'You're over the limit.'

I looked at Carmen.

'So's Jarvis,' I said.

She nodded.

'Got the strategy?' I asked.

She shook her head.

'I'm working on it,' she said. 'Trying for a two-pronged approach. Blenter's contact plus something else.'

I tried to think of something intelligent to say but my heart wasn't in it. To tell you the truth, I couldn't even be bothered to form the right sentences. I was tired, really tired, and it was a relief not to try. I closed my eyes. When I opened them again, Carmen had gone.

Thirteen

I dozed for the rest of the day and into the night. Halfway through it I woke to discover that I was no longer enmeshed in a hammock of pain. It wasn't that the pain had entirely disappeared, more that my mind had snapped back into gear. I realised I'd been bathed in a merciful web of shock that had finally worn off. It was replaced by a memory of the events of the preceding day. I closed my eyes and a parade of people loomed up at me, as if I were watching a movie. I saw Toby gloating about Alicia, my attacker taking his run up for a last kick and Marion Weatherby leaning into an argument with her ex-husband.

The images were distorted – larger than life and inescapable. I opened my eyes and they vanished but the sound track, a confused conglomeration of violence and pain, continued to echo through my brain. I groaned. In his sleep Sam put out a hand and touched my forehead, reassuring me. It helped, but not for long. Every time I tried to return to sleep, every time I stopped controlling my thoughts, the fear returned. I shivered once and then again. Before I knew it my teeth were chattering and I didn't know how to stop them. They went on and on and so loudly that they even made an impression on Sam's sleep. He woke up. Without speaking he wrapped another blanket round me. He sat beside me, holding my hand. I closed my eyes again and this time I slept.

I woke to find light streaming through the windows. Sam

was still sitting beside me. I smiled at him and to my relief the smile came out genuine. Physically I still wasn't in great shape but that didn't seem to matter. I'd fought with demons during the night and they had begun to recede. I knew that it would be a long time, and maybe never, before I could feel the same about walking the streets at night but I also knew that I had begun the healing process. It felt good to be alive. I smiled again.

Sam returned the smile. He leaned down and kissed me. He smelt of soap and coffee and of the things I suddenly wanted to do again.

'You're smiling,' he said. 'That's good to see.'

'So are you,' I said. 'Thanks for last night.'

'Ready for breakfast?' he asked.

I nodded.

'I'll bring it in,' he said.

'No you won't, I'll come out.'

Sam didn't protest. He helped me out of my lying position and he kept a respectable distance from me while I tried to work out if I was mobile. It turned out that I was. I made it to the bathroom by myself and I managed to give myself a bath in stages which allowed me to get clean and the bandages around my ribs to stay dry. I even managed to dress myself, although shoes defeated me.

I got myself to the sitting room, shoeless but elated. While Sam laid the table I made a phone call and an appointment and then I sat down with him.

I was half waiting to see whether my mood would inexplicably crash. It didn't. I drank coffee, I ate some thick Greek yoghurt along with a spoonful of acacia honey and I followed this with a slice of black rye and Gruyère cheese.

I was on my second cup of coffee when the bell rang. Sam went to answer it. I heard the sound of voices in the hallway enquiring after me and I was surprised when I recognised them.

They came into the room in two groups. The first group, Carmen, Elmore and Sarah Parsons, walked in sedately

160

enough. The second lot burst in. It was composed of Kaya, Carmen's daughter, Meg Parsons and her mercifully silent, tottering brother Danny.

Kaya came over to me and gave me a sloppy kiss. Meg Parsons stood on the sidelines frowning.

'You got beat up,' she said in a loud attention-gathering voice.

I smiled a welcome at her and she relaxed a bit.

'Do you have children?' she asked.

I shook my head.

'Well you sure are lucky,' she said in the exasperated voice of a grown-up.

Sarah Parsons looked embarrassed. The rest of us laughed.

'Come and look at Matthew's toys,' Sam said. He led the children's contingent out.

I looked at the adults.

'We changed our minds,' Sarah explained.

'We've been too passive,' Elmore said. 'We've been acting like we're the criminals.'

'We want to fight,' Sarah finished.

'What changed your minds?' I asked.

'He did,' Sarah said, at exactly the same time as Elmore said, 'She did.'

They both laughed. Sarah's mirth went on longer than his. She flung back her head to give rein to it. Then she stopped herself and looked puzzled as if she hadn't been able to express anything other than pain for a long time and wasn't sure she was ready to do so now.

'We met,' she explained, 'in the street. I was on my way to give him hell for putting you on to me and he had come round to tell me that I was letting the memory of Tommy down. We had a blazing row, right there in the street. We saw what was happening – us victims fighting while Jarvis gets off scot-free. So we called Carmen.'

'And she told us what had happened to you,' Elmore said.

'That didn't put you off?' I asked.

Sarah's face took on a far-away look.

'What more can they do to us?' she asked. It was a rhetorical question.

'I contacted Jonathan Blenter's friend,' Carmen said. 'He's willing to start the ball rolling. He's going to suggest that the police investigate a possible insurance fraud run by Jarvis. That will get attention to the case. Then we can come in: if we make a big enough stink they won't be able to ignore us.'

'I've been in touch with the union,' Sarah said. 'Funny, I always left that sort of stuff to my Tommy.'

'You're on your own now,' said Elmore.

'Yes,' said Sarah. There was loss in her affirmative but there was also something else – the beginning of an awareness that maybe she could do more than just survive in a hostile world.

'Let's take the kids out for a treat,' Elmore said.

They went into the other room and gathered their troops. There was the sound of uncontrollable whooping mixed with a cry as the toddler got under the older kids' feet. Then Meg Parsons came back for one brief appearance.

'Can Kaya come to my house?' she said.

Carmen nodded. Kaya rushed in and kissed her. She rushed out again.

'I'll pick you up in a couple of hours,' Carmen shouted after her.

When they'd gone, I looked at Carmen.

'A happy ending?' I asked.

She shrugged.

'Who knows whether we'll get anywhere, but it's worth trying. And at least the two of them are not so defeated by it all.'

'Do you think they're getting it together?' I asked.

Carmen had got up and was walking towards the door. She made a detour past me. She put her fingers on my hair and mussed it.

'Honestly, Kate,' she said. 'You've got sex on the brain.

'I know,' I said, 'And I'm beginning to wonder why.'

I phoned Trevor Plastid and persuaded him to visit me. He agreed without much grace. But he did come on time. He rang the bell at twelve prompt. Sam let him in and then went into another room. By five past twelve I was facing Plastid as he sat opposite me, smoothing the creases on his trousers.

'I do hope this is important,' he said, and frowned. His insignificant face was rat-like, I noticed.

'I'm worried about Alicia,' I said. I told him about the wreath at Pete's funeral. 'I'm scared she may try and kill herself.'

'Why should she do that?' he asked.

'You tell me,' I said.

I had tried it just to see, and I was quite surprised at the result. I had expected that Plastid would toss my remark off. Instead he sat there silent for a moment, thinking of something. He blinked as if to banish the glimmer that had stolen into his eyes. 'Alicia is . . . a difficult teenager,' he said finally.

'With a mother problem,' I said. 'What's between those two?'

'I wouldn't know about that,' he said. 'You seem to be forgetting that I am merely Marion's solicitor.'

'Who's on first-name terms with her.'

'That's not unusual,' he snapped. I thought I might have touched on a nerve somewhere but I was also beginning to wonder whether the man had nerves.

'Known her for a long time?' I asked.

Plastid was growing impatient. 'Of what relevance is this line of questioning?'

'I want to know if you were also Richard Weatherby's solicitor,' I explained.

'I haven't seen Richard for years,' he answered.

'But you were once his solicitor?'

He flicked impatiently at his knee.

'I was the family solicitor. Richard Weatherby left the

country soon after he and Marion parted. I don't believe he's been back since.'

'He's here now,' I said.

It was like I'd dropped a bombshell. Plastid leaned forward. For the first time colour suffused his face.

'He's what?' he asked.

'I saw him at James Morgan's funeral,' I said. 'Talking to Marion.'

Plastid had already half risen out of his seat and my sentence propelled him fully upright. He behaved as if he wasn't completely in control of his actions. He strode to the door and wrenched it open. Something, perhaps the unfamiliar sight of my hallway, helped him regain consciousness. He turned back to me, a weak smile touching his lips.

'I do apologise,' he said. 'You must think me frightfully rude. But I must be off.'

'A man's got to do what a man's got to do,' I said. 'But before you go, tell me one thing.'

'Anything to oblige,' he said.

'Is the Ming still in the piano?'

He looked at me in surprise but I could see that he understood exactly what the question meant. He took his hand off the doorknob.

'I advised Marion at the time that she was being too devious but she felt it was for the best. She felt you might understand if she asked you to find something as valuable as the vase.'

'Rather than some papers?'

'Exactly,' he said. 'Alicia took some very personal documents – without anything but sentimental value.'

'Why blame Alicia?' I asked.

'Because she is the only person who knew where to find the documents.'

'Not necessarily,' I said.

'What do you mean?'

'It's an old bureau,' I said. 'And it's fixed to the wall. I guess it's been there a long time. So her father could have known about the documents.

'Richard?' he said as if he was puzzling something out for himself.

'That's right.'

He didn't comment. He just stood there and let me watch his mind working overtime. A variety of expressions crossed his face; a variety of explanations seemed to supersede them. It was fascinating to watch: it was the nearest I'd ever come to observing somebody talking silently to themselves. Whatever he was working out was complicated but the conclusion he drew was obviously satisfactory. His face cleared: he smiled to himself. He registered my presence. He gave me a half bow and then left the room.

'How was that?' Sam asked after showing Plastid out.

'I dunno,' I said. 'I keep getting the feeling that I'm giving away more than I'm finding out.'

'The mark of a generous woman,' Sam said.

'And a dreadful detective,' I answered. 'I think I'll take a leaf out of Carmen's book.'

'Great idea,' Sam said, moving in close.

'Now, who's got sex on the brain,' I said. 'Remember the ribs.'

At three o'clock I was in Belsize Park. I rang at the doorbell that bore the name of Morgan and waited for James's mother to come and fetch me. She lived in a garden flat in a double-fronted house that would have been magnificent if it hadn't been butchered. But out of one unit had come many. The once spacious hall was boxed off and tacky: windows were cut by walls, and ceiling heights by false floors. Only in the winding banisters and a few remaining ceiling roses could some of the former glory of the place be seen.

Alexandra Morgan had to use sticks to get herself to the door. I heard her making slow and painful progress towards me. I wondered how the lack of mobility affected her life but when I looked at her face I could tell that whatever had happened to her body, her spirit was unbent. Her face was lined with age and with knowledge: grief was written on it as well, but it was a grief that she had taken into herself firmly, so that it had strength in it.

'I'm sorry to disturb you at this time,' I said.

She waved my apology away.

'I have always believed that only through talking can we understand,' she said. 'My son lives in my heart. Why should it detract from his presence to talk about him?' She smiled at me. 'But I am lecturing,' she said. 'it is a habit of old age, a habit to be struggled with. Come in, come in.'

The two of us tottered to her flat. She commented on my uneven gait and I explained a bit about what had happened. She accepted my explanation without comment.

She showed me into a room which was a feast for the eyes. Colours abounded, colours so bright they should have clashed. But they didn't – instead they lent warmth to each other.

She saw me take in the room and she saw my appreciation of it.

'I re-create the sun,' she said. 'It's not to everybody's taste.' She shook her head at my awkward posture. 'Don't stand on ceremony,' she said, and the way she said it made me feel that I'd been unnecessarily coy. 'You look uncomfortable. Sit down over there – the chair is old but the stuffing is strong.'

She watched while I lowered myself gingerly into the chair. She nodded to herself in satisfaction. She left the room and returned very soon after holding an old-fashioned copper kettle. She took it to where a tray had been laid with two cups, a teapot and a matching milk jug. She poured hot water into the teapot. She saw me looking at her and she grimaced.

'Age,' she said. 'I used to believe that the only value in life came from being spontaneous. Now I prepare everything in advance.'

She put the kettle down on a mat that had been laid beside the tray and then she took a step backwards and levered herself into an ugly straight-backed chair with a high seat.

'This way I can get out of it,' she said as she used the large wooden arms to position herself.

She reached over and poured two cups of tea. She handed me one.

'Baeier,' she said. 'An interesting name. Where does it come from?'

'Portugal,' I said and then I saw the doubt in her eyes. 'Lithuania originally.'

She nodded. 'My family, they were Litvaks.'

'Morgan?' I asked.

'My husband's name,' she said. 'I married English.'

She lifted herself up and hobbled to the mantelpiece. She took down a silver-framed photo. She handed it to me. I smiled at the generosity in the face of the bearded man who smiled back out at me.

I saw her looking at me. There was a kind of anticipation in her face, as if she was waiting for me to say something. I wanted to, if only to please her, but I couldn't guess what she wanted. I kept quiet. She used words to hide her disappointment.

'John was a socialist,' she said. 'A union organiser. A Welshman. My mother threatened to stop speaking to me but he was a good man and she wanted what was best for me. He was a good man,' she repeated.

She replaced the picture on the mantelpiece and leaned against it.

'James took after him,' she said in a far-away voice. 'The others, they grew very English, very proper. They are good people in their own way but they're scared of life. They take no risks. We had no stability in our lives and were prepared to gamble. They, with all their advantages, they're scared.'

She walked back to her chair and sat in it.

'But James,' she said, and her voice was stronger now. 'he had our guts. He wanted to make something of life, not just to make money.'

She took a sip of her tea.

'Forgive me,' she said. 'You have not come to listen to the

167

ramblings of an old woman. You have come to discuss James's death.'

There was something in the way she said it that made me pause. I looked at her and in my look there was a question that I didn't want to put into words. I left it up to her to choose whether to answer it. She chose to.

'My son,' she said, in a voice without expression, 'did not fall down stairs by accident. That was not James's way.'

Her choice of words confused me. 'What do you mean, way?'

This time she looked at me before she spoke. It was a strange look and it lasted a long time. I felt as if she was searching for something – something that I couldn't manufacture, something that she expected to see in my face. There was nothing I could do but stay still, praying that I possessed whatever it was she was searching for.

When she spoke again it was if she had come to a decision. 'I am not a fatalist. I have always believed that people possess a power over their own lives even as they live in a society which determines their being.'

I nodded to show I understood and she carried on.

'But sometimes,' she said, 'I have watched people heading towards their fate as if nothing would stop them. I have watched them struggling with the forces around them at the same time as they are helping those same forces towards their goal.'

Her voice rose as she spoke until its richness filled the room.

'I have seen this happen to people who have given up,' she said, 'to people who don't think they can win, to people who no longer want to win. And I saw it happen to my son.'

'What do you mean?' I asked.

She paused and she thought hard about it. She was no longer deciding whether to tell me but rather concentrating on how best to do it.

'You know Alicia Weatherby,' she ventured.

I nodded.

168

'What do you think of her playing?'

'I'm not an expert,' I started but stopped myself when I saw the look of impatience cross her face.

'I thought it was brilliant but inconsistent,' I said.

That pleased her. She leaned forward, excited.

'Exactly,' she said. 'Alicia has ability, she has fire, she has an instinctive understanding of the pieces she chooses to play – especially the more dramatic ones. But she is inconsistent, her playing is undisciplined. A common fault, you could say, in one so young. Discipline, we could guess, is what she has still to learn and what she could be taught.'

She paused and shook her head.

'But it is not like that with Alicia.' She shook her head again. 'She has not come from the right background to win this struggle with herself – to discipline herself to her music – to give up her genius to her development. Alicia is good for her age but a truly great musician cannot afford to rely only on her wits: she must harness her skill to her training.'

Again there was a pause. This time when she resumed, her eyes were moist.

'I know all this,' she said, 'because I watched my son go through the same thing. I watched him battling to overcome his impatience and his arrogance. In his case, he succeeded. I know what it cost him. And because I know this I also know that Alicia has something in her that will prevent her from winning the battle. Alicia will never succeed in becoming a first-class pianist.'

I had been following her argument closely, searching for its destination. Irrationally, I felt let down. I had anticipated from this wise old woman, if not a solution, then at least a hint of one. Instead I had been given her thoughts on genius and what tames it. Okay, so Alicia would never make it to the top – that I was prepared to accept. But so what?

I looked up from my thoughts to see her watching me. She gave me a smile that showed that she understood my confusion.

'This I know about Alicia,' she explained. 'And my son

knew it too.' She let the sentence hang there for a while before continuing.

'My son felt very strongly about pushing people too hard. He felt that his problems came from such pushing. He vowed that he would not put another young person through the mill of false expectations. And yet he was prepared to take on Alicia even though he knew that her talent was flawed. We must ask ourselves why.'

She leaned back as if she had finished. Her face took on a calm look of having done all she could, of having finished the job.

'The question is why,' she said again.

She blinked with finality. She didn't have to say anything more or to look at me again. Her intentions were clear – she had taken me as far along the path of her own understanding as she was prepared to go. If I wanted to reach the end, I would have to do so on my own.

I tried my damnedest to understand what she was getting at. I closed my eyes because I thought that it might help. It didn't. I got up and limped aimlessly towards the mantel-piece. Out of the corner of my eye I saw that Mrs Morgan was watching me intently. I made myself ignore her scrutiny. I was thinking as hard as I had ever thought before. It was almost there – the solution. I knew it was. All I needed was to bring it to consciousness. I looked blankly in front of me.

That's what did it. I was standing in front of John Morgan's picture as I tried to free my mind so that I could dig into its recesses. I was so close that the picture blurred. I stepped back a fraction and looked again. And in that moment, I understood. I looked away for a second and then back at it. It was the same – now that I had seen it I knew it for the truth.

I held the picture up. 'She looks like your husband,' I said. 'That's what you were trying to tell me – Alicia looks like her grandfather. That's why I thought I recognised James – not because I had seen his photo in a magazine but because I saw Alicia in his face.'

The woman breathed out slowly, as if she'd been holding her breath.

'James was Alicia's father,' I stated, just to make sure.

'It is the one thing that James felt he had to keep secret from me,' she said. 'And I respected his wishes. I never told him I knew. And so I could not tell you – not straight out.'

She pulled herself upright. When she next spoke, her voice had changed. It had lost its colour and its strength. It had become older and shakier. She stared at the ground in front of her.

'James and Richard Weatherby were best friends,' she said. 'I never approved. Richard Weatherby had life too easy. He walked with a smile on his face but underneath I always thought that there lurked a hard side, a side that should not be tangled with. But my son chose his own friends and I did not interfere. And then James did something of which I was deeply ashamed. He started an affair with Marion – his best friend's wife.'

She looked up and her eyes brightened a bit.

'I am not against permissiveness,' she said. 'I do not think sex is to be taken too seriously. But I disapproved because what it indicated was that my son had taken on the values of the Weatherbys. What had been a strong friendship no longer meant enough to him. Of that I disapproved. But still I said nothing, hoping that it would stop.'

'It didn't?'

'It did,' she corrected. 'But only after Alicia was born. I had assumed when I heard Marion was pregnant that she and James had forsaken each other. I guessed wrongly that she had entangled herself with my son as one last bid before she settled for motherhood. I was deeply relieved.'

'And how did you find out the truth?'

'I went to see the baby. My son requested that I do so and it was a natural enough act. I had spent some social time with the Weatherbys. I went willingly. I felt that it was James's way of telling me that he had finished with Marion. After I realised what had happened I realised that James asked me to go because he wanted me to reassure him that Alicia was not his child. I could not do so. I looked into Alicia's face and I saw my James as an infant. When he grew older he changed – he did not look so much like his father – but as a baby he was the spitting image.'

'What did you do?'

'It was not my business and I kept my peace.'

'Did the others know?' I asked.

'My experience of life is that human beings have a great capacity for fooling themselves. Richard Weatherby – I don't think he ever knew. He could not have concealed his feelings if he had. My son, he wanted to know and yet he didn't. He persuaded Marion to have the three of them, himself, her and the baby, given blood tests. Marion kept the results to herself. I overheard her saying that they proved that Richard was the father. I would have done the same had I been in her shoes. Her relationship with James was no longer viable.'

'Did James believe her?'

'He seemed to. Or he fooled himself into pretending that he did.'

'What happened to change that?'

'Alicia happened,' she said. 'Alicia started to play. She played well. She played, in the beginning, because Marion encouraged her, out of some perverse sense of justice, I suppose. James followed her progress from afar, hoping, I think, that she would grow bored. But she did not. Long after Marion lost interest, Alicia continued to develop musically. She had nothing in her life but music and therefore music took over.'

'And James couldn't keep away?'

'In the end, no. And in the end it proved his undoing.'

I looked at her and asked something that had been on the tip of my tongue since she had started talking about James's death.

'If you believed that James was murdered,' I asked, 'why didn't you try to force an investigation?'

'He was my son,' she said. 'But she is my granddaughter.

172

Whatever happened was not her fault. I did not want her punished for it.'

'I don't think she did it,' I said.

'If I could believe you,' she said, 'that would give me a great deal of peace.'

'I'm trying to prove it,' I said. 'Or Alicia will live her life under a cloud of suspicion. Either that, or she will choose not to live.'

She heard what I said, and she understood what I meant. She threw me an uncertain glance.

'I did not see Alicia very often,' she said. 'Until my son took me to hear her playing. It was then that I knew he was reviving the old pain. There was nothing I could do to stop him. And perhaps I did not want to.'

'Why not?' I asked,

'Because of Alicia,' she said. 'Because I saw that she is a girl driven by an agony of some kind. An agony she herself does not understand.'

'Do you?' I asked.

She threw her hands up in a gesture of hopelessness.

'There are many things that can torture a human being. Unspoken, intangible things. Bring them to the light and they can be dealt with. But in the dark they are always frightening. Alicia struck me as a child who lived in the shadow – trying to come out of the night but without success. I do not know what caused the terror. I could merely hear it in her music.'

I nodded. I too had heard it.

'When did Richard and Marion part?' I asked.

She wrinkled her brow as she thought back.

'Eight years ago,' she said. 'Richard left in a hurry. Nobody knew why. One day he was gone. It was then, I think, that Marion encouraged Alicia to play the piano. Perhaps she was trying to keep the child's mind off the divorce.'

'Perhaps,' I said.

I got up. I walked over to her and offered her my hand.

She took it and held it for a fraction of a second.

'Thank you,' I said.

'It is for me to thank you,' she said, 'for trying to rescue Alicia. I could not save my son: perhaps his child will survive. I wish you luck.'

'Thank you,' I said again.

I walked towards the door. She made no attempt to follow me. Only as I reached it and was about to go out, did she speak again.

'I have begun to think,' she said. 'That I was too hard on James. I drove him forward because I said nothing. I knew that his involvement with Alicia would do him no good. I should have spoken out.'

I looked back at her, sitting straight and proud in her chair. 'You did what you thought best,' I said. 'The way you had been taught.'

She laughed to herself, a low mirthless laugh. 'Which does not mean I did the right thing,' she said.

Fourteen

I went straight to the office. I went there because I needed a base. I was confused. I'd found out so much, I had enough of the missing pieces to get a hint of the puzzle and yet I still didn't know what it meant.

I grunted in response to Carmen's bright hello. 'Nothing?' she queried.

'On the contrary,' I replied. 'I learned a lot. But I don't know what it means.'

'Well I have something to add to it all. I've got some good news, some bad news and some very interesting news. Which do you want to hear first?'

'Let's try the good.'

'She's reappeared.'

'Who has?'

Carmen clicked her tongue. 'Your protégée,' she said. 'Alicia Weatherby. Your friend Toby phoned to say that he'd found her.'

'*My* protégée. *My* friend. Why've they all become mine suddenly?' I asked.

This time Carmen whistled. 'Get you,' she said. 'What's up?'

'Nothing much,' I said. 'Just two murders and an unhappy girl. Where did she go?'

'Out of London,' Carmen said. 'We were right. She was toying with the idea of killing herself, but in the end she didn't have the courage. She said she had nowhere to go, so

Toby persuaded her to phone her mother. She'll take the train back tonight.'

'Umm,' I said. 'So what's the bad news?'

'Marion Weatherby phoned. Given that Alicia's been found she would like to dispense with your services so . . .'

'She can't do that,' I interrupted, 'I've got a contract.'

'So,' Carmen raised her voice, 'she requests your presence at her place where you can discuss the situation and, she is convinced, come to an arrangement acceptable to both parties.'

'I'd better go,' I said.

Carmen held up her hand to stop me. 'Not so fast. You haven't heard the interesting news yet.'

'Shoot.'

She looked at me proudly. 'I've tracked Crant down. You know, that policeman.'

'Oh,' I said.

She wasn't going to allow herself to be put off by my lack of enthusiasm. She held up a sheaf of papers.

'It's interesting. Very interesting. Because Crant shouldn't have been interrogating you at all. He has nothing to do with murder investigations. You see, for the past ten years, Crant has been part of the . . .'

'Drug squad,' I finished for her.

Carmen's face fell, but not for long. Bemusement took the place of disappointment.

'How did you know?' she said.

'I didn't,' I said. 'I guessed partly because of the way I was arrested and held without charge. If the police really thought I'd done it, they would have played by the rule book. When they didn't I began to wonder why. I guessed the charges were an excuse to keep me out of the way. Somebody bought some time while they made sure Alicia wasn't arrested for the murder of James Morgan. I was too difficult a suspect so they found another – Pete. They murdered him and left his body lying next to a do-it-yourself suicide note.'

'Where does Crant fit in?'

'I don't know how much Crant knew of all this. I suspect that he's none too bright and merely carries out instructions.'

'And the drug squad?'

'Just a guess. Pete was killed with heroin which was one clue. The other was the way I was moved through police stations. I don't think Crant was merely keeping me away from you – he was also hiding his actions from his superiors. He'd only go out on a limb like that if there was big money involved. What else but the squad?'

'Not bad,' Carmen said.

'It doesn't help, though,' I said.

'Why not?'

'Because Pete was killed to save Alicia Weatherby. And why did Alicia need saving?'

'No reason,' Carmen said, 'unless . . .'

'Exactly,' I said. 'Unless she pushed James Morgan. And I think I've found the motive.'

I told Carmen what I'd learnt from James' mother. She listened in silence until I'd got to the end of my story. By the time I'd finished she was worrying, just as I was, about what we were going to do about Alicia Weatherby. I almost smiled at the irony of it all. We had come a long way together on this case. We were finally thinking alike, Carmen and I, and yet neither of us felt like celebrating.

Carmen interrupted my thoughts. 'You think James told Alicia that he was her father and she couldn't bear it?' she asked.

'Something like that,' I replied.

'Doesn't seem like a good enough motive for murder.'

'I suppose she did it in a fit of temper. She probably didn't mean to kill him. And I've worked out something about Alicia's past. It explains a lot. It explains why she's such a mess. It explains why she's buried all memory of Richard Weatherby – it even explains what Toby said about the time he went to bed with her.'

Comprehension showed on Carmen's face. 'Oh no,' she said.

'Afraid so.'

Carmen frowned. She thought it over. When she had finished she shook her head. 'No way, Kate,' she said with conviction. 'It still doesn't make sense. Where would she find the strength to push James Morgan so hard? And what could he have said to bring something that she had so long buried to the fore?'

'I dunno,' I said.

The reply didn't satisfy Carmen. She carried on thinking out loud. 'From what you told me, whatever happened in the past the trouble's now between Alicia and her mother. Correct?'

'I suppose so.'

'Good. We also know that Richard Weatherby, the man she thought was her father, had disappeared from her life. It's quite possible that, if James Morgan really did tell her he was her father, she would have been pleased. I mean, he was offering to look after her. He was offering her another option.'

'Yes,' I said.

'Talkative, aren't you?'

I kept my mouth shut. She gave an exaggerated sigh. 'Fact three,' she continued, 'there's drugs involved. It's not about sex after all.'

I slumped into a chair. 'I've worked it out and yet none of it makes sense . . .' I started. And then it clicked. I finally understood. I jumped up excitedly.

'Don't be so sure,' I said.

She stopped, surprised to have provoked more than one word out of me. She looked at me keenly. 'What do you mean?'

I didn't answer. I was too busy thinking.

'You're up to something,' Carmen said. 'What are you thinking?'

'I'm thinking about a surfeit of fathers,' I said, and noticed with detachment how slowly the words came out. 'I'm thinking about a girl in a lot of trouble. And a mother who presumes guilt in her daughter. And some missing papers which have only just gone missing. And I'm thinking about who gets blamed. And who is really to blame. And how I just fell into the same trap.'

'And what do you get?' Carmen asked.

'I tell you one thing,' I said. 'I don't get drugs. Or Alicia. See you later.'

I left the office on a high – a high of having worked out something that had been nagging at me for a long time. But halfway to the Weatherbys' I came down to earth. I thought I knew what had gone on and yet knowing didn't solve anything. Knowing didn't tell me what to do with the information. 'Turn back,' a voice inside me said, 'it's not for you to meddle.'

I almost followed that voice. I almost did turn back. But before I could I remembered something else – the last thing that James' mother had said to me and I remembered the hollowness of her laugh. I thought that if I turned back now I would be making the same mistake she had made. Alicia Weatherby was a girl who had been lied to all her life. That was the pattern and that's what trapped her. I had it in my power to cut through the lies: how could I refuse? I carried on.

The doorman was at his usual post. He looked subdued. I threw him a smile which he pretended not to notice. I walked to the lift, pushed the button and waited. The lift took a long time to arrive. By the time it did another piece of the puzzle had slotted into place.

I turned to face the doorman.

'How long have you worked here?' I asked.

'Fifteen years,' he said.

'You weren't drunk that evening, were you?' I asked.

He looked at me.

'You saw who it was that went in,' I said. 'You recognised him.'

'I don't know what you're talking about,' he said in a monotone.

'It's not worth it,' I said. 'Whatever you were paid. This is a serious business. It's murder that's involved.'

He swallowed but he remained still.

'You recognised him,' I repeated.

This time I got a vague nod. I copied the nod before stepping into the lift.

Marion Weatherby answered the door.

'No Eva?' I asked.

'I gave her the evening off. Servants,' she said and she stressed the word and looked at me to see I got her meaning, 'can hear more than is good for them.'

I ignored the dig. I was in no mood for it. Nor did I want to wait for her while she reluctantly closed the door. I made straight for the living room and entered.

It was still as big as when I'd first seen it but it wasn't as empty. There were three people sitting in it – Alicia Weatherby, Trevor Plastid and one other man. He was the one who got up when I entered. He strode over to me and shook my hand.

'Richard Weatherby,' he said. I noticed that his voice was tinged with an Australian accent.

He was acting like the host. He gestured me towards one of the couches and he remained standing until Marion had entered and we'd both sat down. Trevor Plastid, who'd made it halfway up at my entry, sank back again. He smiled at me. Alicia was keeping her own counsel. She had not taken her eyes off the floor when I came in and she didn't do so now. I looked around me. I noticed the blue Ming vase on the mantelpiece.

Richard Weatherby moved to sit next to Plastid so that both men were lined up to my right. Marion Weatherby, sitting opposite us and next to Alicia, made sure Richard had settled himself before she started the ball rolling.

'We really are extremely grateful for all your efforts on our behalf.'

She paused at the end of the sentence as if waiting for me

to say something. I think she was hoping I'd do the decent thing and bow out before further unpleasantness. I sat and waited. She threw Plastid a glance which was poignant with disapproval and then she continued. 'Trevor saw fit to issue you with a contract. I want that contract terminated. After all, Alicia has returned to us.'

Marion looked meaningfully at her daughter beside her. Alicia still didn't budge. She kept her eyes on the floor and her hands clasped in her lap. She looked terrible.

It was the sight of Alicia that kept me in my seat. The inner voice that told me not to interfere, to let things stand as they were, was stilled when I looked at her. I knew as surely as I have ever known anything that she was a girl in urgent need of help. I was the only person who could offer it. I cleared my throat. I turned to Richard.

'Why did you come back?' I asked.

'I had business to attend to.'

'And a funeral,' I said.

His eyes didn't move. I looked into them and saw how blue and how cold they were. As they locked on to mine I felt again the edge of what I had experienced ever since I'd met Alicia and Marion – an edge of something sinister and secret. Richard carried it too, and seeing that helped me confirm what I had guessed.

'Naturally I'd go to James' funeral,' he said. 'He was my friend.'

'Who you no longer saw,' I said.

Richard smiled. 'I could hardly do that. I was in another continent.'

'Air transport's a wonderful thing these days,' I said.

'I've been busy.'

'For more than eight years?' I said. 'Too busy even to see your daughter? Or was that part of the divorce settlement?'

'I can't see what business this is of yours, Miss Baeier,' Marion chipped in. 'Our divorce settlement was our affair.'

'It would be, if it wasn't for Alicia. And the matter of two murders.'

'What murders?' Marion Weatherby said. She'd gone all perky on me – she might have been asking about a movie.

'The killing of James Morgan,' I said. 'And Pete.'

'Surely, Miss Baeier,' Marion said in an exasperated voice, 'that is a matter for the police.'

'For Crant?' I asked.

There was a movement beside me and the sound of an intake of breath but when I turned round Richard Weatherby was still. He was looking at Alicia so intently that he missed my scrutiny.

'And there's the burglary,' I said. 'What about it?'

'I am prepared to let the matter drop,' Marion said magnanimously. 'After all, I am insured.'

'Against the loss of some papers?' I asked. 'Against the theft of the results of a blood test which was done some eighteen years ago?'

This time the movement beside me was strong and hard. This time when I looked at Richard Weatherby I saw that his weathered face had gone a deathly shade of white.

I didn't have time to see what he would do next. Instead, it was Alicia who attracted attention. She stood up so abruptly that she almost fell forward.

'Can I go?' she said. 'Can I go?'

Her words tumbled out in a plea for release that sent shock waves through my bones: they were words of desperation – the final exposure of a long buried fear.

Marion Weatherby got up and stood next to her daughter. She made no effort to touch her.

'Of course you can, darling,' she said gently. 'Go and lie down.'

As if in a trance Alicia turned to leave. She began to walk haltingly towards the door.

I felt torn as I watched her progress. Again my decision stood in the balance and again I had to tussle with myself. But as I watched her, things moved back into sharp focus. I knew what I should do.

It was her slow pace that encouraged me. I could see that

Alicia was desperate to get out. I could also see that something was holding her back and it was to that something that I appealed.

'Don't go,' I said.

'Miss Baeier,' Marion protested.

'Don't leave now, Alicia,' I went on. 'You'll never know.'

She took two more steps towards the door – two more indications of the struggle inside her.

'You have to face it,' I said. 'You can't bury it any more.'

She stopped where she was. She turned towards us. Her expression was stony, her face locked into immobility, but she had made up her mind. She came back and sat herself down, making sure to arrange her skirt round her. She looked at me expectantly. I looked back at her.

'I don't know what you mean,' she said, in a voice that belied the statement.

'Something happened to you,' I said. 'A long time ago. Something that you buried inside yourself and that returns to haunt you.'

'I don't know what you mean,' she repeated.

I ignored the desperation in her voice. I had to, in order to continue.

'You won't ever be rid of it,' I said, 'unless you face it.'

She buried her head in her hands so that when she spoke her voice was muffled.

'I can't,' she said.

'Why not?'

'I just can't. I try and try but I can't remember. Help me.'

She raised her head and leaned towards me as if she wanted to disappear into my lap. I smiled at her, trying to ground her in that smile. As I did so I was conscious of how still the adults around me had become. I felt their anticipation in that stillness and, again, I knew I was right.

But being right didn't make it any easier. I cleared my throat. 'For a start, tell me what happened the night James was murdered.'

When she spoke she did so without hesitation, even

though her voice sounded like it was coming from a long, long way away.

'I talked to James,' she said. 'About my music. He said he would take me on. Then he left me to think about it. I waited for Pete to come and see me. I waited a long time. I was expecting him. I got scared when he didn't come.'

'So you went to find him?'

She nodded.

'And saw them there?' I asked.

Again she nodded.

'James and Pete?'

This time she didn't nod. She kept completely still for a moment and then she shook her head, once, twice, a third time.

'Pete was on his way back,' she said. 'He had almost reached me. James was still at the top of the stairs. He was with someone, someone else.'

'Who?'

'I don't know,' she said. 'It was dark. I couldn't see. They were talking and I didn't listen. I was worried about what James might have said to Pete. I was worried about what Pete would do. I didn't see. I don't know.'

Her head shake began again. This time it didn't stop. It went on rhythmically from left to right and back again. It was as if Alicia was trying to shake the thoughts from her mind but doing so without any hope that she would succeed. I got up and went and knelt in front of her. I held her hands in mine. She didn't show that she had registered my move but she did stop shaking her head.

'What happened next?' I prompted.

'He pushed him,' she said. 'They were arguing and the man pushed James.'

'And then?'

'James fell. He lay there. The man ran down the stairs and bent over him. And then he left. I wanted to go and see whether James was all right but Pete stopped me. He said it was dangerous. He said the man might be there, waiting for

184

us. Pete said he knew what to do about it. He said I should keep out of the way. He made me go back to the common room and stay there. I did what he asked me. But then he never came back and I couldn't bear to wait there any longer. I went out. I had to see, to see whether James was alive. I went to look.'

'And that's when I found you?'

She nodded.

'Why did you tell me you'd done it?' I asked.

Tears started to roll down her cheeks. She opened her mouth to say something, but nothing came out.

'Why?' I asked.

The tears kept coming. She tried to choke them back but there were too many of them for her to control.

'I felt it,' she said. 'I felt responsible. I thought it was my fault. It was my fault. It was me. I did it.'

Her voice rose as she spoke. 'It was me,' she repeated over and over again in a tone that sent a shiver down my spine. I was looking at an eighteen-year-old but I was hearing the voice of a toddler.

Marion Weatherby went up to her and hit her once, in the face. Abruptly Alicia stopped talking. She froze.

'Can't you see what you're doing to her?' Marion shouted. 'Alicia is very highly strung. I cannot permit this.'

'If you don't,' I said, 'you will be allowing the whole sad mess to carry on just like you have for years. Is that what you want? Another tragedy but this time with Alicia at the foot of the stairs?'

'I don't know what you mean,' Marion protested.

'It's too late to keep pretending. You know what I mean. You've always known. And knowing meant that you wouldn't let Richard see Alicia, couldn't bring yourself to trust her with your men friends, pushed her to play the piano to prove something to yourself and then turned her towards the violin because the proof would make you as culpable as you had convinced yourself *she* was.'

Marion didn't say anything. She sat there, white-faced and

still – so still that I couldn't even see the rise and fall of her chest as she breathed. I waited for her to speak. But Marion did not speak and it was Trevor Plastid's voice that rang out over the silence.

'You're full of accusations, Miss Baeier,' he said, 'most of them incomprehensible. I suggest you get to the point.'

'I'll try another way,' I said to Marion. 'Tell me why you assumed that Alicia had killed James Morgan?'

'She told me she had,' Marion said.

'She told me that,' I said. 'She told you only after you assumed it. Why make that assumption?'

'I was worried,' she said quickly, 'I didn't know what I was saying.'

I grimaced to show her how unconvincing she was. She didn't like that. Her voice lost its modulation and came out in a kind of screech. I wondered whether, in that loss of control, there wasn't some measure of relief. Marion had kept the lid on this for so long – maybe she too needed it to come out.

'You tell me why,' she shouted. 'If you know so much.'

I looked at Alicia as I started to talk. I wanted to watch her face, to know how far I could go and when I should stop.

'Your mother assumed you killed James Morgan,' I said, 'because she knew that James was your biological father.'

Alicia looked up but not at me. She was looking at the man, Richard Weatherby, who was sitting next to me. He didn't move a muscle.

'And,' I continued, 'she thought that you would have good reason to want to kill your father.'

'James had never done anything to her,' Marion protested.

'James hadn't,' I said, 'but the man she had always been told was her father, Richard Weatherby, had. You kept the secret of Alicia's paternity so long that in your unconscious you conflated the two men together. You thought Alicia had reason to kill her father and that's why you so easily blamed her for James' death.'

'Nonsense,' Marion Weatherby said.

186

I thought about that, and I nodded my head. 'You're right. It's even worse. You hold Alicia responsible for what happened in the past. You think it was her fault, as does she. Both of you have lived with the assumption of Alicia's guilt – lived with it and not talked about it so that it has grown unfettered and expanded into the space between you. And because of it you believed that Alicia could kill.'

'Nonsense,' Marion Weatherby repeated. This time she didn't even try to make it sound as if she meant it.

I'd been watching Alicia but my hope that she would tell me when to stop had been unfounded. She stayed with her eyes fixed on Richard. They were opened wide as if she was trying to use them to extract something from him.

'Why did you do it?' she asked.

She didn't wait for a reply. She turned to her mother. 'Why did you let him?'

Marion Weatherby covered her ears with her hands.

'I don't know what you mean,' she cried. 'I don't know what either of you means.'

'Why?' Alicia repeated.

Richard Weatherby was the one who replied. His voice was so soft that it was a strain to catch his words. 'Don't blame your mother,' he said, 'she didn't know. It was me, I was the one who did it.'

He looked at Alicia but then lowered his face to avoid her eyes.

'I was lonely,' he said. 'I wasn't in control of myself. And you, you were so pretty, so full of life, so eager to please me. I couldn't help myself. And you seemed not to mind.'

'You killed me,' Alicia said.

'Don't say that,' Richard pleaded.

'You killed me,' Alicia continued, 'with your touch and with your lips. And I didn't even know it. All my life I've felt like I was evil. I was evil, because you touched me.'

Richard put his head in his arms and he sobbed. 'I didn't mean to,' he said between the sobs.

'Pull yourself together, Richard,' Marion said coldly. She

had taken her hands from her ears and she was sitting upright. I saw her strength again and I saw how mixed with coldness that strength was. Trevor Plastid saw it too – beside me I heard a sharp intake of breath as if he was in pain. I heard the sound, I registered it, but I had no time for it.

Marion's coldness worked on Richard. He stopped crying. He looked up and he looked at Alicia through eyes that were full of pleading. She got up and moved away – trying to escape his gaze and his confession.

'I didn't mean to hurt you,' he said. 'I was weak. I needed help.'

'And I was a child. You were my father.'

A kind of pathetic eagerness filled Richard's voice.

'But don't you see,' he pleaded, 'I'm not your father. James Morgan was. I know what I did was wrong, but it wasn't incest.'

Alicia shivered. I knew how she felt.

'How did you find out that James was her father?'

'I looked at the blood test,' he said. 'I always knew Marion was hiding something from me. For years I've lived with my shame. For years I've had to stay away from my baby. I sent others to England when the business required it. And then I could stay away no longer. I had to come back. And I had to check what I'd always suspected, hoped, was true. I decided to look. I needed to know. I needed to know that what I'd done wasn't so . . . ugly.'

'So you found Alicia's keys at the school and you came here,' I said.

'No,' he said.

'And you killed Pete because he saw who you were. He knew how to find you – you were his dealer. He was in a position to expose you for what you did. Because he saw you kill James Morgan – the man who you thought had ruined your life by taking Marion from you.'

'No,' he repeated.

'You can deny it,' I said, 'but not for ever. There's too much evidence against you. The doorman here saw you come that night – you paid him to keep quiet. I bet the porter at the school could recognise you as having attended that evening. One of Pete's friends knows you for his dealer. And when the police are told all this I can't see Crant standing by you – not for a murder charge. He'll throw you to them, anything to save his own neck. And when he does that, the so-called suicide note will turn up and your writing will be all over it.'

'No,' Richard Weatherby shouted. He got up and took a step towards me. His hands were shaking, his features were distorted. I shrank back into my chair.

Fifteen

I never knew what Richard might have done because he didn't get the chance. Instead somebody else leapt into action and they did so decisively.

Trevor Plastid was on his feet at once. In one swoop he had come behind Alicia. He grabbed her by the throat. He was holding a gun to her head.

'Nobody move,' he said.

We all froze. And we looked at him.

He liked that. He smiled.

'Very clever, Miss Baeier,' he said. 'You collected all the evidence. Pity you got the wrong man.'

He started edging towards the door, dragging Alicia with him. Richard Weatherby took one step as if he were about to follow.

'Don't do it,' Trevor Plastid said. 'Remember, I've already killed two people. One more makes no difference.'

'Why?' I asked.

He nodded pleasantly at me but the nod was badly timed. The suave solicitor had gone, perhaps for ever. What I had once thought of as his insipid features hardened. His face was transformed.

'Money,' he said. 'And my good reputation. Why else?'

I could think of another reason, but it wasn't the time to say so. I knew that I needed all my inner reserves to stay calm. I forced myself to look at him, but I found it almost impossible to face those eyes. They glinted with vengeance, with something approaching insanity.

I sat quite still, my heart pounding with anxiety. Plastid had killed twice and I had good reason to suspect that Alicia's death would be of little meaning to him. I watched him. He was still edging backwards, scared to take his eyes off us but anxious to escape. Alicia was stiff in his grasp but she had no choice but to go with him.

As I watched them, I saw the door move. At first I thought I had imagined it but then it moved again. It opened a fraction. I tore my eyes away from it.

'Why James?' I asked, frantic for conversation. 'You killed Pete because he knew who you were and because he saw you with James. But why kill James Morgan?'

'Simple really,' Plastid gloated. 'He deserved it. Look what he did to Marion. She confided in me, you know, when she became pregnant. And afterwards as well. She told me about the blood tests. I was her only real friend, the only one she's ever had. She made me listen to all the details. She needed a shoulder to cry on, and how could I refuse? She was besotted with James Morgan. She thought he was special. She wanted someone exotic, someone artistic. I knew she wouldn't have looked at a mere solicitor. She was fooled by Morgan, even after he ditched her.' Plastid stared into the distance, remembering his disappointment. 'She could have done so much better. She could have chosen . . .' He stopped in mid-sentence, as if he had caught himself saying something intolerable. He tightened his grip on Alicia. 'I never wanted to hurt you,' he said to Marion. 'I only ever wanted to protect you.'

The four-legged crab that was the two of them took one more step towards the slowly opening door.

'But that was all so long ago!' I said. 'Why kill him at this point?'

'Why don't you understand?' Plastid asked plaintively. 'I had to get rid of him. He knew about me. Pete told him. I heard him say it. Morgan was one of those people who liked to play god. When he left Alicia he met Pete on the stairs. He started giving Pete a moral lecture on the dangers of drugs

191

and Pete was incensed. He was a stupid brat, that one. I heard him boast to Morgan that even the most respectable people were involved in drugs. Pete named me. Morgan might have told Marion.'

'But Trevor, I never kept in touch with James,' Marion protested.

Plastid acted as if he hadn't heard. 'I couldn't take the risk. Morgan deserved to die.'

The door was now fully open and out of the corner of my eye I saw a flash of colour as Eva crept into the room. She moved quietly towards the two figures.

Plastid had no idea she was there but I knew that at any moment he might turn to the door and would see her. I had to distract him from doing that. I had to give her time. I prayed silently to myself as I kept my eyes on Plastid as if fascinated. I could hardly concentrate on what he was saying. But I had to keep him talking.

'Pete had always known who you were,' I repeated.

Plastid grinned at me.

'Don't be naive, Miss Baeier. Pete was a junkie. Who was going to listen to him? As you have so rightly deduced, I had police protection. But it would only stretch so far. James Morgan was too respectable. He would have scared Crant.'

'Why take the papers?' I asked. 'The blood-test proof?'

'Oh, I didn't do that,' he said. 'Richard did. I had Alicia's keys all right, but then, you see, Marion had never changed the lock. Richard had his own keys.'

'So the doorman never saw you?'

'As a matter of fact he did,' Plastid said. 'I'd come in earlier. I wanted to check on something.'

'On Alicia,' I said. 'You wanted to get her. You thought she saw you kill Morgan.'

He shrugged. 'As you wish,' he said. 'And now, I must be going.'

He dipped his head at us, as if in a last farewell. When his eyes alighted on Marion, his face saddened.

'I'm sorry,' he said. 'It should have been different.'

That gave me the opportunity to look towards the door again. I saw that Eva had almost made it. I understood what she was planning to do, I even thought it had a good chance of working, but I knew that she needed a few more seconds to do it.

'Wait a minute,' I said. The words came out in a shout but Plastid didn't seem to notice and I talked quickly to cover it up. 'One last question. What were you doing at the concert?'

'Ah yes,' he said. 'That was unfortunate. But I went for Marion. She asked me to. I didn't understand why at the time but now I know that it was because Richard was back in town and she was scared that he and James would meet again and, after all these years, finally talk about Alicia's paternity.'

He moved back one more step.

'I shouldn't have gone,' he said and looked puzzled, as if he was trying to work out why he had. He never got the chance.

He still had the puzzled expression on his face when Eva picked up the blue Ming vase and brought it crashing down on his head. The puzzled expression stayed there but his hand dropped. The gun fell to the floor. He crumpled and thudded down on top of it.

Alicia was pulled down with him. She yelped once but then lay there, pinned down by the weight of his unconscious arm. Richard Weatherby rushed up to her. He put out his hand.

'Don't touch me,' she said.

'But Alicia, I . . .' he started.

'Don't touch me,' she said. She was breathing as if she were in shock, but I wasn't too worried. For the first time since I had met her, Alicia's voice sounded as if it came from inside her. And more than that, it sounded like a voice that belonged to an eighteen-year-old and not a sophisticated adult or an injured child.

'Call the police,' I said to Richard. 'And do it now.' I smiled at Eva who was in the process of extracting the gun from under Plastid's body.

It took what seemed like an age for the police to arrive. It took even longer to explain what had happened. When we'd managed they carted Trevor Plastid away. They didn't look pleased and I reckoned that he was in for a rough time. I didn't think his involvement with Crant was going to give him anything but sorrow from now onwards.

Richard Weatherby made one more attempt to speak to Alicia but she ran away and locked herself in her room. When I knocked she wouldn't reply. Marion was no use: she sat unmoving on the sofa for what seemed like hours. The police gave up questioning her when they saw the blank look on her face. Eva called her doctor who gave her a shot and packed her off to bed.

That left Richard Weatherby. He, in contrast to Marion, had a compulsive desire to keep talking. He wanted to confess. He latched on to the senior policeman and started apologising for his past actions as if they were the only point at issue. In some sense, I suppose he was right, but the police force don't think that way. They lost interest as soon as they understood that he was gabbling about something that had happened so long in the past. They had a double murderer on their hands which pleased them greatly. But they also had information about corruption in their ranks, and they gave the impression that they wanted to get out of the place as soon as they could to deal with it.

So Eva and I were left with the remnants of the man Richard had once been. I almost felt sorry for him. He seemed to have aged so much. I looked at him and I could hardly detect the strength that I had noticed when I saw him at James Morgan's funeral. I didn't think he would ever find it easy to live with what he had done now that it had come to the fore.

Eventually Eva and I managed to persuade Richard to go back to his lonely hotel.

'I couldn't help myself,' were the last words I heard from him.

I turned to Eva. 'Do you think he'll kill himself?'

She shrugged. 'Doubt it,' she said.

I held my hand out to her. She took it and smiled.

'What is it with the English?' she muttered. 'They're all crazy.'

'Must be the climate,' I said. 'See you around.'

She nodded. My last sight of the Weatherby household was of her on the doorstep waving at me, the bright colours of her clothes standing out against the white carpet. I found myself hoping that I would see her again.

I went home and found Carmen and Sam waiting for me.

'Let's go for a walk,' I said. 'I need air.'

We drove to Primrose Hill and walked to the top. It was a clear morning and I could see London stretched out far beyond us. It looked deceptively clean in the early morning light. I told my friends what had happened as I breathed in the crisp air.

'So it wasn't to do with sex after all,' Carmen said when I'd come to the end.

'Or about Alicia. Her only contribution was to hire me and she did that to mess up her mother's relationship with Gordon Jarvis. That's the irony of Alicia's life. For half of it she bore the guilt for something she never did – something she was involved in but was in fact peripheral to.'

'What do you mean?' Sam asked.

'The adults were in trouble and she was the casualty. It was nothing to do with her. They just used her. Just like now. Everything seemed to centre round Alicia when in fact it was nothing much to do with her.'

'I wonder whether Richard was right,' Carmen mused. 'I wonder whether Marion really didn't know what he was doing to Alicia.'

'Of course she did,' I said. 'Somewhere. But she didn't want to admit it to herself. So she wafted through life in a haze of uppers and downers and charities and Gordon Jarvises. She couldn't help Alicia because she couldn't help herself.'

'And now?'

'Who knows?' I said. 'Maybe she and Alicia can work it out. Maybe Alicia can be free. Maybe not.'

In the distance I saw a milk truck making slow progress along Primrose Hill Road. Then something struck me. I turned to Carmen who was following.

'In a way it was about sex,' I said. 'I just got the wrong people.'

'What do you mean?'

'Plastid was in love with Marion,' I said. 'Had been for years. Maybe if he wasn't he wouldn't have gone to the concert. He must have known that Pete would be there. Maybe he wouldn't have pushed James if he hadn't known that James and Marion had been involved enough to have a child. I get the impression that Marion used Plastid as a repository for her confidences. She's a selfish woman, with incredibly bad judgement. She had no idea that she was fanning the flames of Plastid's jealousy. And it was jealousy that led him to such a drastic course of action.'

'I suppose you could call murder drastic,' Sam teased.

'It's no worse than what Jarvis did,' I said. 'He did it for profit. And what will happen to him. He'll get off scot-free.'

Carmen shook her head.

'He won't,' she said. 'He'll be prosecuted. The police have no other choice now we've given them the proof. Gordon Jarvis is a man in a lot of trouble.'

I squeezed Carmen's hand.

'We did well,' I said. 'It was rough but we did well.'

'We did,' she answered. 'So what's next?'

'I know what I'll do,' I said. 'Take me home.'

I left the two of them on my doorstep. I went inside and shut the door firmly. I picked up my alto from the stand on which it had lain untouched throughout the Weatherby investigation.

I strapped it round my neck, walked to the stereo, and put on 'Trouble in Mind'.

And then as 'Backwater Blues' came on, I accompanied Archie Shepp and Horace Parlan, blowing hard and sweet against their music, blowing it all out and away from me.

. . . .

Also of interest:

Gillian Slovo

Death by Analysis

When psychoanalyst Paul Holland is found dead in mysterious circumstances, private detective Kate Baeier is called in to investigate. The hunt for the killer leads from elegant Belsize Park to the streets of Hackney, where Kate is drawn into a web of intrigue and a powerful police cover-up.

'Takes us right into the simmering streets of North London.' *Bookseller*

'Gripping...you'll never guess whodunnit. Don't miss Kate's next assignment.' *Literary Review*

Crime fiction £5.95
ISBN 0 7043 4018 6

Marcia Muller
Edwin of the Iron Shoes

Featuring Sharon McCone, Private Investigator.

Sharon McCone, Private Eye. Single, strong, scrupulous and sharp. Drawn into investigating San Francisco crime, she fights corruption and supports the powerless.

When a small-time antique shop owner is found murdered – stabbed with a bone-handled dagger from one of her own displays – Sharon McCone's first case begins . . .

Crime fiction £5.99
ISBN 0 7043 4364 9

And watch out, too, for all the later, hugely popular, Sharon McCone mysteries:

Ask the Cards a Question £5.99
ISBN 0 7043 4365 7

There's Something in a Sunday £5.95
ISBN 0 7043 4312 6

The Shape of Dread £5.95
ISBN 0 7043 4313 4

Trophies and Dead Things £5.99
ISBN 0 7043 4314 2

Where Echoes Live £5.99
ISBN 0 7043 4315 0

Pennies on a Dead Woman's Eyes £5.99
ISBN 0 7043 4337 1

Wolf in the Shadows £5.99
ISBN 0 7043 4389 4

Meg O'Brien
The Daphne Decisions

Launching the Jesse James mystery series . . .

Murder doesn't get much colder than on the icy shores of Lake
Ontario, where Jesse James is on the trail of a property fraud that
has led to a string of costly accidents . . .

**'Five stars! Here is a mystery with verve, style, wit and a
gutsy new heroine who is always good-hearted if often
wrong-headed. This new heroine will quickly become an
old favourite.' Carolyn G Hart**

Crime fiction £5.99
ISBN 0 7043 4360 6

And watch out for Jesse James in:

Salmon in the Soup £6.99
ISBN 0 7043 4361 4

Hare Today, Gone Tomorrow £5.99
ISBN 0 7043 4366 5

Eagles Die Too £5.99
ISBN 0 7043 4381 9